The Dark Brand

Center Point
Large Print

**This Large Print Book carries the
Seal of Approval of N.A.V.H.**

The Dark Brand

LP
W
DEROSSO
2014

H. A. DeRosso

CENTER POINT LARGE PRINT
THORNDIKE, MAINE

This Center Point Large Print edition
is published in the year 2014 by arrangement with
Golden West Literary Agency.

The text of this Large Print edition is unabridged.
In other aspects, this book may vary
from the original edition.
Printed in the United States of America
on permanent paper.
Set in 16-point Times New Roman type.

ISBN: 978-1-62899-163-5 (hardcover)
ISBN: 978-1-62899-164-2 (paperback)

Library of Congress Cataloging-in-Publication Data

DeRosso, H. A. (Henry Andrew), 1917–1960.
The dark brand / H. A. DeRosso. — Center Point Large Print edition.
pages ; cm.
ISBN 978-1-62899-163-5 (hardcover : alk. paper)
ISBN 978-1-62899-164-2 (pbk. : alk. paper)
1. Large type books. I. Title.
PS3507.E695D37 2014
813'.54—dc23
                                                    2014014347

CHAPTER 1

The cell door clanged shut behind him like a knell of doom, and on the moment he felt more alone and forsaken than ever before in his life. In the opposite cell a man grunted and stirred. From outside, beyond the cell window, came the sounds of hammering on the new gallows, and it seemed to him that he stood, cold and desolate, in a world apart. He shrugged, and two steps brought him to the barred window.

There lay Santa Loma, the dusty main drag and a couple of crooked side streets and alleys, the false-fronted buildings in the heart of the town and the smaller dwellings beyond, somnolent in the sunlight of late afternoon. He watched without feeling, for this was not his town. He was one of the lost, seeking what the restless wind sought, except that now he was caged like an animal while the wind still ranged joyous and free.

The sound of sawing came and only then did he lower his eyes and look at the gallows. He could not understand why it affected him like his, for the grim structure was not for him.

The man in the cell across the corridor coughed once and cleared his throat. There was a moment's silence and then the hammering resumed.

5

To get his mind off the sounds outside, he got the makin's out of his shirt pocket—the sheriff had removed all else from him and concentrated on rolling a cigarette.

"Could I have the borrow of that, friend?"

The voice, though it was soft, startled him but he finished his job of rolling a neat, tight cylinder and popped it into his mouth. He pulled shut the Bull Durham sack and walked to the cell door.

The man stood, one hand dangling outside the bars. He was slim with a dark, pleasant face and a smile that was friendly, but also lost and sad.

After the man thanked Driscoll for the Bull Durham, bitterness edged Driscoll's voice. "Don't they even furnish you with tobacco in this tank town?"

The man laughed quietly. "I've been smoking kind of heavy today. I told Longstreet—he's the sheriff—I was out of tobacco and he said he'd fetch me some, but Longstreet forgets. He forgets pretty convenient sometimes. And, by the way, the name's Tennant," he said, tossing back the tobacco sack.

"Mine's Driscoll."

Driscoll put away the makin's and stood awkwardly, like a child wanting to blurt out an awful, embarrassing question.

As though Tennant had read his mind, the man said quietly: "Yes. The gallows is for me. . . ."

6

• • •

Driscoll stood, back to the wall, staring bitterly at the floor.

"What did Longstreet nail you for?" Tennant asked softly.

A moment's resentment flared in Driscoll, then was gone. "I was caught with some cattle I didn't have a bill of sale for."

"Oh?" Tennant said. "Are you one of those boys I'd heard were operating out of the Sombras? If so, Longstreet's been after you for a long time."

"That's right."

"How'd he treat you?"

Driscoll rubbed his wrists where the manacles had chafed cruelly. "Not bad," Driscoll said, poker-faced.

"Watch him," Tennant said. "I wouldn't doubt there's a streak of Apache in him. If he hasn't touched you yet, he will. Watch him."

"Why? Did you find out the hard way?"

"He's worked me over, all right," Tennant admitted, "but not because I wouldn't talk. I never tried to hide anything. He worked me over because he's poison-snake mean."

Tennant grew silent. After a long time he asked: "Have you ever killed a man, Driscoll?"

The question startled Driscoll. He shook his head.

"I see him all the time," Tennant said quietly. "I'm sorry I killed him. I cried over it afterward.

7

But if I had the whole thing to do over again and it meant killing him again, I'd do it the same way."

His world was not as dark as he had once believed it was, Driscoll told himself.

Tennant was silent while the hammering on the gallows increased in tempo. "I guess I'm scared," he said, "but in a way I'll be glad to get it over. I knew when I did it that it couldn't be any different."

Driscoll said, "This man you killed—didn't you try to plead self-defense?"

"I had no quarrel with the man. We weren't enemies at all. He was a little fellow with just enough strength to raise a gun. He was a teller in the bank in Fort Britt. The bank I robbed . . ."

From outside, above the hammering and the sawing, came the sound of children's voices, shrill and sweet. A man tiring of the calling and laughter, shouted angrily, and the children fled, their shrill sweetness suddenly gone.

Tennant said, finally, "I knew I'd be recognized, and for that reason I didn't even wear a mask. I was known in the bank because I'd borrowed money there and they thought nothing of my walking in. They thought it was a joke even when I pulled my gun. I had to rap old Sloane across the head. When he dropped unconscious they knew I meant business. They put all the cash they had in the gunnysack I took with me. I thought they were real scared and wouldn't give me any more trouble, with old Sloane knocked out.

"I went outside and got on my horse. The teller came to the door with a pistol. He pinked me in the arm. Then he got a bead on me and I knew his second shot would tag me good. I had to get him before he got me. When he dropped I knew I'd hit him in the heart."

In the sheriff's office a door clanged and two men shouted but the words were indistinguishable.

"I got away, all right," Tennant went on. "I hid the money and rode to my ranch and I was there waiting when Longstreet came. He had no reason to work me over but that night when we were alone here in the jail, he worked me over good. For the teller, he said it was, for the man I'd killed. And Longstreet loved it. He cared nothing for the teller."

The sawing and the hammering had resumed. And Driscoll couldn't restrain the question: "Then why did you do it? You don't look like a bank robber to me."

Tennant withdrew into silence. At last he said, "Do you have a family?"

The question startled Driscoll. Lately, he had begun to suspect that here lay the cause of his bitterness, his aimless tumbleweeding. He could rot here in this cell and no one would care or grieve.

Driscoll shook his head.

"Well, I have," Tennant said quietly. "You get a poor calf crop and your water just about goes dry and you borrow money to drill a well. Two dry ones, and you have to borrow again. Your wife wears clothes that she mends over and over. Your son wants red-topped boots and you can't even buy him a stick of candy. You want your kid to have what other kids have. You want him to grow up and get on in the world. Well, my kid will have it some day, the legacy I'll leave him. That money I stole and hid. It will all be his one day. I'll hang in the morning, but all that money will be my Billy's. They promised me that if I'd tell where the money was hid I wouldn't die. But no one's taking it away from Billy. So . . ."

Driscoll went over to the window and looked down and saw that they were finished with the gallows. The men looked at their handiwork with pride. Driscoll saw Tennant lying on his cot with an arm over his eyes.

Driscoll sat on the hard edge of his bed, rolled and smoked a cigarette. When finished, he flicked the butt at the window but it struck a bar and fell back, still smoking, on the floor.

A key rattled in the lock on the cell-block door. Driscoll saw the tall, cadaverous length of Sheriff Ira Longstreet pass through the door and come with clanking spurs. Longstreet gave him one look from pale yellow eyes. Then the sheriff was rattling Tennant's door.

"Rise and shine, Tennant," Longstreet yelled. He tossed a sack of Bull Durham as Tennant roused.

"Thanks, Sheriff," Tennant said.

"Glad to do you one last favor, Tennant," Longstreet said, "but don't ask for no more."

Tennant stuffed the bag in his shirt pocket. His face looked drawn; he wet his lips. "My—my family. When do I get to see them?"

"Your wife was around this afternoon but I told her to come back this evening. One visit is all she gets with you."

"You rotten skunk," Tennant said.

"Mind your tongue, boy. Don't forget that when I put the noose around your neck. I can make it quick, or I can make it long and mean."

There was the silence again. A group of riders went by outside, the jingle of bit chains sounding sweet in the early evening.

"For myself," Tennant said, "I'm not asking anything, but this is for my boy. He's only eight, Longstreet. He needn't know what's going to happen to me."

"If he's got eyes he's already seen the gallows."

Tennant made a choked sound. "Me and Hazel have talked it over. She promised to keep the boy away from everybody so that he can't find out what's happened until it's over. Is that asking too much, Longstreet?"

"What if he asks me about the gallows? What am I to say?"

"Tell him it's for me," Driscoll said quietly. He sat, tense and angry, on the edge of his bunk.

"Eavesdropping, Driscoll?" There was no rancor in Longstreet's tone or hint of annoyance.

"What should I do?" Driscoll said. "Hold my hands over my ears?"

The pale eyes watched without expression. "Chipper, aren't you, boy? We'll get some of that vinegar out of you." He turned to Tennant. "I'll have some grub sent in to you. After that, I'll send your family in."

"What about me?" Driscoll asked.

Longstreet stopped. "Don't tell me you're hungry, too, Driscoll?"

It was hard for Driscoll to keep his anger down. "At least, send me in some water. I haven't had a drop since I've been in here."

Longstreet was chuckling as he passed through the door and locked it.

Tennant sat on his cot with his face in his hands, making soft, choked sounds. Driscoll sat and listened and felt like bawling, himself . . .

CHAPTER 2

It was night now. A lantern flickered smokily from the corridor ceiling.

Driscoll stood at his window. The shadowed gallows loomed below against the stars, and the lights of Santa Loma shone golden and gay. Across the corridor, Tennant paced restlessly in his cell.

Driscoll was standing there, lost in thought, when he heard the key jangle in the lock and the iron door swung open. Tennant grew abruptly still.

Driscoll watched them enter—the pale-faced woman leading the boy by a hand. Tennant made a choked sound that was echoed by the woman. Then they were embracing through the bars. Into these last, precious, desperate moments, Driscoll could not bring himself to intrude. So he stared out into the night and tried not to hear the whispers, the last intimate endearments.

"Daddy, when are you coming home?" the boy's voice said.

He had to listen, even against his will.

"Soon, son," Tennant said gently. "I'll be out of here very soon."

"How come they keep you in here so long? We need you at home. A door come off—"

"Hush, Billy," the woman whispered.

"But it did, Ma. The door to—"

"Don't bother Daddy with things like that."

"I'll fix it when I get home, Billy," Tennant said.

"Is that the man who's gonna be hung?"

Driscoll stood half-obscured in the shadows but he could see them clearly. They were all watching him now, Tennant and his wife with distress and anguish on their faces, the boy with awe and pity.

"Hush, Billy."

"I asked Mr. Longstreet about the gallows and he said it was for that man over there."

"Hush, Billy," the woman said, a catch in her voice.

The cell-block door opened. "Time's up, Miz Tennant," Longstreet called.

The last embrace took a long time. The woman's head turned once toward Driscoll but her eyes stared past him into the depths of hopelessness and despair.

They passed through the door and it clanged shut. The sound echoed in the desolate, forsaken air. Then it, too, vanished.

Driscoll emerged from the tortured depths of sleep with a feeling of anger and bitter hate. The cell block was dark. When he rolled his eyes back he could see a star or two through the barred window. He made a wild guess. A break? On the moment he felt his sympathy rush out to Tennant and he found himself praying, Dear God, let him get away, for the boy.

He sensed someone watching him from the door of his cell. He feigned sleep and soon the shadow moved before Tennant's cell.

"Hssst! Tennant."

Tennant's drowsy voice said, "Who's there?"

"Come closer. I want to talk to you."

Longstreet! Driscoll thought.

"Quiet," the sheriff said. "Don't wake Driscoll. Now listen, you fool. I'm offering you your life."

It was as though the whole world were holding its breath. Then: "Come again?" There was no life in Tennant's whisper.

"You want to die? Do you really want to hang?"

In the darkness outside something snapped but the sound was so faint it could have been a trick of the imagination.

"Can't you let me be?" came Tennant's soft, tormented voice.

"You don't believe me, eh? Well, you just take it easy, boy. You can be free this very night. By morning you can be miles away, laughing at that gallows outside. You hear me, boy? Of course, there's a price. And I swear to God in heaven you'll go free if you'll pay it."

"The bank money?"

"That's right, boy."

15

"You know what I told the judge and the prosecutor. I haven't changed my mind."

"I don't blame you. If you turned the money over to the law, they'd change your sentence to life in prison. That's not much choice, is it, boy? The rope is better than that because it's quicker. But I'm giving you your freedom, your life. Think on it, boy."

"Go to hell, Longstreet."

"Now don't get your hackles up, boy. I'll make a deal with you. The bank reckons it around thirty thousand. How about a deal? Fifty-fifty. Doesn't that sound fair?"

"You think I'd trust *you?* I wouldn't trust you if you swore on a stack of Bibles as high as the highest peak of the Sombras."

"All right then. Think on this for a change. It's me who's gonna put that noose around your neck in the morning and spring the trap. I can fix that rope so that it snaps your neck so quick and easy you won't feel a thing or I can fix it so you'll hang there a long time, choking to death. Your hands will be tied and your legs and while you're strangling you'll keep trying to get at that rope tightening around your neck but you can't move your arms. You'll try to kick and thrash and can't budge—"

"Stop it," Tennant hissed. "If there's such a thing as coming back from the grave, I'll do it, Longstreet. I'll come back and kill you."

"You do that, boy. Meanwhile, pleasant dreams."

In the darkness, Driscoll could hear Tennant's labored, anguished breathing . . .

From his window Driscoll could see the festive crowd gathering. There were horsemen and there were rigs, many of them dust-covered as though they had come a long way. Some of the people had brought lunches with them and they sat in their wagons, eating and chattering.

Angrily, Driscoll turned and crossed to the cell door. There he stopped, sick and shaken, and watched Tennant sitting with his face in his hands.

Tennant lifted his head once and saw Driscoll and smiled wanly. Tennant's face was pale and drawn but no fear showed in his eyes.

A key scraped against the lock and Tennant gave a start. The cell-block door opened.

"Rise and shine, Tennant." Longstreet entered the cell block, followed by three deputies armed with scatter-guns. Longstreet unlocked Tennant's cell.

"I'm supposed to read you the writ of execution," Longstreet said, "but it's just a waste of time."

Tennant was standing straight, shoulders squared. He shook his head.

"Turn around, then. I've got to strap your arms."

17

Longstreet drew the bonds tight. When Tennant faced around, his features were taut with pain. Longstreet grinned.

"All right, boy. On your way."

Tennant walked on rigid legs. As he passed Driscoll, Tennant threw him one look. Driscoll started to reach out a hand and Longstreet lashed down with his pistol barrel. Driscoll groaned and clutched his aching wrist.

Tennant's eyes said that he understood. Then Tennant and Longstreet had passed and it was not until the sheriff's back was beyond the door that Driscoll remembered to spit after him . . .

The voice of the crowd died to a murmur as Tennant and the deputies appeared. Tennant reached the gallows steps, squared his shoulders and with steady stride ascended.

Driscoll found that he could not tear himself from the window as Longstreet guided Tennant to the center of the trap. Then Longstreet strapped Tennant's legs. A black hood was dropped over Tennant's head, and the sheriff fitted the noose around the doomed man's neck, tightened the knot, and stepped back.

The thud was audible even up here on the second floor of the combination courthouse and jail. There was a gasp from the crowd, a sound of horrified enchantment. The hooded man swayed gently in the space between the dropped trap and the ground. Longstreet was marching pompously down the gallows steps. Some of the crowd was beginning to leave.

Driscoll cursed aloud, his lips a thin line in his colorless face . . .

He lay on his back on the cot with both arms thrown over his eyes, trying not to remember, and fell into an uneasy doze.

There came a jangling from outside and voices raised in impatience and anger. He opened his eyes, turned his glance toward the cell door and saw Longstreet there, face dark with anger, fingers rattling the door.

"What does it take to wake you?" Longstreet snarled. "The trumpets of judgment day?"

"You low-down dog," Driscoll said wearily. He sat on the edge of the cot and stared balefully at the sheriff.

"You want me to come in there, boy?" Longstreet said gently. "You want me to come in there and lay hands on you?"

Lethargy dropped swiftly from Driscoll. He gripped the edge of the cot fiercely, toes pressed to the floor to send him flying forward.

"Do that, Longstreet," Driscoll said. "Please, just do that."

Longstreet said, "There'll be plenty of time to take care of you. You'll still be here."

"When do I get to eat? I haven't had a bite since last night."

"Sorry, you sort of slipped my mind. I'll have some grub sent in. Later."

"How about some water now?"

"We'll talk first," Longstreet said. "Then you'll get water."

"Oh, go to hell," Driscoll said and lay down.

"Boy?" Longstreet rapped softly with a fingernail on an iron bar. "You better go along with me. There ain't a man or beast in town who knows you or gives a damn about you. I can throw your key away and no one will care. But you'd care, boy. I'd see to it that you would."

Longstreet stood, his pale yellow eyes empty of expression, his seamed pointed face like that of a coyote.

All at once Driscoll felt beaten, sullen. Hunger gnawed, thirst scratched. He sat and stared at the floor.

"What do you want to talk about?"

"That's better, boy," Longstreet said. "You'll find me an easy man to get along with if you quit fighting the bit."

"What do you want?"

"The names of your pals. Where their hide-out is, where you all drove those rustled cattle. Who you sold them cattle to. I want to know everything, boy."

"I worked alone. There was no one in with me."

"Pshaw, you think I just started sheriffing, boy? I been sixteen years in this job. You tell me straight, now."

Driscoll wet his lips. "I lone-wolfed it."

"Look at me when you say that, boy."

Driscoll's eyes locked with Longstreet's. "I lone-wolfed it."

"You're a damn liar, boy."

"All right," Driscoll said wearily. "You know more than I do."

"You fighting that bit again?"

"I lone-wolfed it."

There was a pause. Longstreet made a sound of insufferable exasperation.

"You're trying me, Driscoll. Don't do it."

Driscoll stared at the floor.

"I know you had help," Longstreet said after a while. "There were at least three of you, riding out of the Sombras at night and running off them cattle. I caught you but not your pardners. Who were they, Driscoll?"

Driscoll did not speak.

Longstreet sighed. "You're making it tough only on yourself, boy. You think your pardners wouldn't squeal on you if they were in your fix?"

"I've got no partners."

"I know. You lone-wolfed it, didn't you?" Longstreet sighed again. "How thirsty are you, boy? You want some water? If I give you water, will you tell me then?"

Driscoll said nothing. Which was worse—Tennant's image there, or the clawing thirst in his throat?

"You just wait there, boy," Longstreet said.

He left and was soon back with a tin dipper dripping water. Driscoll started eagerly, then with an effort checked himself. Longstreet laughed softly.

"You talking, boy?"

Driscoll glared silently at Longstreet.

"No?" Longstreet said. "Well, just to show you my heart's in the right place, I'll give you water anyway."

The liquid caught Driscoll in the face before he could duck. It splattered over him, choking him, wetting his shirt. He sat and gasped and brushed wetness from his eyes.

He began to tremble from pent-up fury. "I'll get you, Longstreet. I won't deny stealing those cattle because you caught me with them but the worst the judge can do to me is send me to prison. He won't hang me. Prison, yes, maybe a long time, but the day will come when I ride back to Santa Loma. Not so much for what you've done to me, Longstreet, but for other reasons. Remember that, Longstreet. Remember it good."

Longstreet hefted the empty dipper in his hand, yellow eyes aglow. Then he laughed, a somber sound. "Dream on, boy, dream on," he chuckled.

The sheriff walked away. The cell-block door slammed shut. Now there was the aloneness again, and the vision of Tennant and his family. And the gnawing, convulsing hate . . .

CHAPTER 3

Three years later, Driscoll drew rein and looked down on the eastern flank of the Sombras. Here the world fell away in slopes and breath-taking precipices, spotted by green clusters of scrub cedar and juniper, and a meadow here and there, and a winking of the sun on a ribbon of creek or slice of pool, and the hills far below running into the horizon, and the one hill topped with tiny, toy-like buildings that was the town of Santa Loma.

His blaze-face black stirred restlessly, anxious to get under way again, and he reached down and patted the horse's neck.

A bitter stir of memory came to Driscoll. It was here in the isolation of the Sombras, in their barren and somber canyons and escarpments, that he'd hidden out by day and by night ventured forth to steal. Whatever made me do it? he thought as the dregs of recollection sickened him. Whatever soured me to make me do things like that? I know now I could never steal again, not because I've been punished, but because there has been a change in me, a very great change.

Tennant? I've never forgotten you—or your wife and kid.

He rode on and the air grew warmer. He took off

his jacket and tied it behind his saddle. The prison pallor on his face was being covered by the brown of the sun.

When he came upon the first cattle, a small bunch of white-faces grazing about a pool, he reined in the black and watched with a sense of nostalgia. The cattle spooked and ran off into some timber and he grinned at the sight and for a moment the world was very bright and buoyant and then the darkness of recollection came, the reason he was returning.

Don't let it get you like this, he told himself. She's probably married again and has forgotten all about him, except maybe a thought now and then. And the boy, too, he might remember, but only a little. And that's the way it should be. You remember because for three years you had nothing to do but lie alone at night, remembering. But her and the boy, something must have come along to help them forget.

But still he wondered . . .

He rode down the main drag at a walk, the black's hide caked and mottled with sweat and dust. Eyes watched him, from open doorways, from windows. A stroller on the street turned to stare after him. There might be recognition here and there but nothing startling, nothing to kindle excitement, he thought. After all, three years had passed and all he'd been was a penny-ante rustler. He had not had his neck broken in a gallows-drop in the open area next to the courthouse and jail.

The area beside the jail was still open; no one had built there. The gallows, of course, was gone; they had torn it down and carted the lumber away even before sentence had been passed on him. Now just the barren ground was there, hard, red earth with a brave weed sprouting here and there, and no trace at all where the gallows had stood.

It was not until the black snorted and tossed its head that he became aware he had reined in at the entrance to the courthouse, almost expecting to see Sheriff Ira Longstreet come clanking out. Perhaps Longstreet was no longer sheriff. Perhaps Longstreet was dead.

He rode on down the main drag, keeping his eyes straight ahead of him, until he came to Mackintosh's saloon. He dismounted and tied the weary black to the rail.

His spurs worried the quiet of the place and a man looked at him from a table in a far corner, then looked away without interest or recognition. Driscoll ordered a cold beer and drained the foaming glass with three prodigious swallows, then stood relishing the prickling sensation in his throat and the way the beer settled, soothing and cool. He belched and ordered another one.

The bartender drew this one and then stared at him. "Haven't I known you from somewhere?"

Driscoll stared down at his beer and shook his head. "No," he said truthfully.

"I swear I seen you some place. But I reckon you'd know. Like the feller says, 'The customer's usually right.'"

Driscoll took another sip of beer and his uneasiness grew. Yet he owed nothing to anyone. His debts had been discharged in the sweltering, lonely hell of the Territorial prison. He wore no manacles or irons. Still the feeling would not go.

He took another sip and was beginning to feel a little better when the sound came that froze him, that caught all his insides in a giant, squeezing claw.

The sound was that of clanking spurs.

He heard the swing doors part and stay thrust aside as the man paused there. Then the spurs started their protest as the man moved in and Driscoll forced his head down.

The spurs stilled beside him. He heard the heavy, indrawn breath.

"You're Driscoll, aren't you? The man who did that rustling in the Sombras three-four years ago?"

The bartender's eyes lashed at him and held. The eyes in the far corner picked him up now and probed with a fierce, knowing intensity.

"I thought it was you riding past. The pen took some suet off you, didn't it?" The chuckle was soft, malevolent. "Look at me, boy."

Driscoll stared at the long, cadaverous face, a trifle leaner now, the yellow, mocking eyes. A big-boned hand tapped softly on the bar.

"Answer me."

"I'm Driscoll."

The yellow eyes probed and searched. "What you come back to Santa Loma for?"

"I'm just riding through."

"You sure you didn't come back for something?"

I'd like to kill you, you mean sidewinder, Driscoll thought. Maybe that's the real reason I came back, not for her and the boy.

"What would there be for me to come back to?" he said aloud. "There's no one in this town that means anything to me."

Longstreet did not answer the question. The star was a pale, silvery scar against the bright crimson of his shirt.

"Will you have a drink on me, Driscoll?"

Driscoll stared, all but open-mouthed.

Longstreet smiled faintly, a slow, lazy crinkling of the lips, like the idle, tranquil grimacing of a panther. "I really mean it, Driscoll. I was hard on you three-four years back, but you were asking for it. I keep law and order in my county. Criminals can expect no mercy from me. Ride the straight and narrow and I don't bother you. I was hard on you because I was trying to get you to tell me who your partners were. You never did say."

Driscoll watched the bartender take his glass and bring it back foaming full.

Longstreet touched his glass to his lips. "It was

all right, though. Arresting you scared your pals off. Anyway, the rustling stopped."

"I had no partners," Driscoll said wearily.

"That's right. You lone-wolfed it." Longstreet laughed, then sobered as he stared at Driscoll's waist. "I see you're packing a gun."

Driscoll's head rose with instant resentment. "I served my time. There's nothing says I can't wear a gun or ride anywhere any time I want to. I've paid for what I did."

"All right," Longstreet said. "Like you say, you can ride anywhere any time you want to. So you do just that, boy. You keep on riding right out of Santa Loma and out of my county."

"You can't put the run on me for nothing at all."

"You call being an ex-convict nothing?"

Driscoll felt a white flame eating at the edges of his brain. "Look, Longstreet," he said, "if I've still got some punishment coming for what I did three years ago, you arrest me right here and now and charge me. If not, then you leave me alone. But don't you threaten me."

Longstreet said blandly, "I'm just telling you for your own good. The smart thing for you to do is ride on and try your luck some place where you're not known. I get cause to throw you in my jail again and you'll think your last tour was a Sunday School picnic. Think on that, boy."

He pushed back from the bar and walked away, spurs clanking.

CHAPTER 4

He told himself it was the mulish stubbornness that had been a part of him as long as he could remember. And a certain measure of pride. He had just about decided to leave this country forever and then this had turned up. He had never liked an ultimatum or anything that smacked of one. He might go under but he would not yield.

He put up the black at the livery and then got himself a room at the St. George. He ate in a small cafe and then, with the night shadows thickening and a wind blowing hard off the Sombras, went up to his room. He took off his shell belt and hung it and the holstered pistol from the bedstead. Then he took off his boots.

Lying there on his back on the bed, smoking and staring up at the shadows seeking to obscure the ceiling, he felt the anger and resentment ebb. A vast weariness descended on him.

In the morning, he told himself. I'll saddle up and ride on in the morning. I shouldn't let Longstreet get me like this. Why take the chance of getting myself into some real trouble just because he rubs me the wrong way? New places, new faces, a look over the farthest hill. That's for me. In this fashion he began to drowse.

He sensed the change in the town the moment he reached the lobby early in the morning. The clerk's eyes picked him up with curiosity and probing. His own glance sharpened and hardened and the clerk looked down in quick embarrassment. Driscoll tossed his key on the desk.

"Leaving us, sir?" the clerk asked.

"That's right."

"Any forwarding address—to send your letters?"

Driscoll stopped and came around slowly, eyes full of a quick anger. "I won't be getting any mail," Driscoll said and walked outside.

As he started down the street it seemed that every eye in town was singling him out and watching him. All at once he was not sorry that he had decided to leave this town. There really was nothing here for him anyway, not with this suspicion like a shroud about him, under constant, stealthy surveillance. Freedom in Santa Loma was for him an illusory thing. He had better leave while he could.

He rode out of town at a trot, leaving his contempt and disgust in the swirl of dust raised by the black. Goodbye, he thought savagely, goodbye to meanness and greed and filth. You'll be a long time seeing me again.

He was leaving without having accomplished the mission he had returned for. But I don't even know her, or the boy, he told himself. I saw them only that one time. I didn't even speak to them.

They've certainly forgotten me by now. And if they do remember, it would make them remember Tennant, too. So it's best if they forgot everything, him and me and that gallows. So ride on, Driscoll, ride on.

He came upon the horseman quite suddenly. The trail he was following dipped into a draw and as the black clambered up the other side and over the lip of the arroyo the rider was there, waiting.

Driscoll reined in the black sharply and dropped his hand to his pistol. The other noted this and held up a detaining hand while a smile spread his mouth.

"Easy, friend," the man said in a quiet, soothing voice. "I didn't aim to startle you. I saw you coming and thought I'd wait for you."

Driscoll kept his hand on his pistol. "Why?" Driscoll's voice was harsh, clipped.

The man moved a hand slowly and carefully to his shirt pocket and drew out a sack of Bull Durham and dangled it from his fingers. "Empty," he said with the smile still wide on his mouth. "Could I have the loan of a smoke, friend? It's still a long way for me to Santa Loma."

A little of the tension flowed from Driscoll. He took his hand off his pistol and passed his own Bull Durham over to the other.

"Thanks, friend," the man said, and began to build a cigarette.

The man finished pouring tobacco, drew the

sack shut with the string held in his teeth and then offered the sack back to Driscoll. The moment he reached for it Driscoll recognized the thing that was not right. The man's horse, a gray, was wet with sweat as though he had been ridden hard. Therefore, this was no chance meeting, but a planned interception.

Driscoll let the sack drop and stabbed his hand for his pistol, but even as he did so the voice whipped out at Driscoll's left.

"Hold it as you are, Driscoll, or you'll get a slug smack in your heart . . ."

They did not mean for him to get away. They bound his wrists to the saddle horn and tied his ankles underneath the black's belly. Then they started off, one of them leading the black, the other riding behind.

They would tell him nothing. They closed their ears to his angry demands and queries and when Driscoll saw that his questions availed him nothing, he lapsed into silence and began studying the back of the man leading the black.

Driscoll was sure he did not know the man behind, the short, chunky fellow who had borrowed the tobacco. But something about the man ahead, the tall leanness of him perhaps, or a mean shiftiness in his glance, reminded him unpleasantly of Longstreet. Try as he might, however, he could not place the man and abandoned himself to a sullen resignation.

The sun was high when Driscoll spied some ranch buildings ahead. His captors made for these without veering. They passed a few white-faces wearing the Bar Cross Bar brand, the same as that on the two men's horses.

They untied Driscoll's wrists from the horn but did not free his hands. They undid the ropes binding his ankles and told him to step down.

The tall man, who seemed to be the leader, finally spoke. "Don't you know me, Driscoll?"

Driscoll shook his head.

"Don't you remember me at all?"

Recognition lurked in Driscoll's mind but never quite came through.

"I'm Otis Hunter," the tall man said. He hitched a thumb in the short man's direction. "That's my partner, Frank Boyd." A faint smile played about Hunter's thin slash of a mouth. "I can understand why you wouldn't remember us. I hope, for your sake, that your memory is better in another matter."

Exasperation mingled with anger in Driscoll. "Will you tell me what this is all about?"

"Hold your horses, Driscoll," Hunter said. "We're coming right along to that and once we get there I don't think you're going to like it." His glance narrowed again. "You remember the day Jim Tennant was hung? You remember Longstreet's three deputies?"

Driscoll nodded. "You. You were one of them."

"That's right. I wasn't a regular deputy. I just volunteered for the hanging." He paused and Driscoll almost expected him to smack his lips. "I can understand why you wouldn't remember me. But I've remembered you, Driscoll. I've remembered and waited for you for three long years."

"How did you know I'd be back?"

Hunter laughed, an expression of scorn. "So that's how it's going to be, is it, Driscoll? Well, you listen to me. I'll ask you but once. I don't expect you to tell me but if you do, you would save yourself a lot of grief. And if you don't, we're prepared to make you. Chaw on that a minute or two."

Driscoll was suddenly aware of his heart pounding. "Tell you what?" he asked.

"You were in jail with Tennant the last night he was alive. I imagine the two of you talked some?"

"We did. He was pretty blue. After all, he was to hang in the morning."

"And he did hang," Hunter said. "And the money he stole was never found."

Silence filled in. "Well, Driscoll," Hunter said at last, "why did you come back to Santa Loma? You've got no one here. Everyone knows you for a thief and an ex-convict. Why come back?"

"If I told you you wouldn't believe me."

"I'd believe the truth, Driscoll."

"And what would you call the truth?"

"The place where that thirty thousand dollars is hidden."

The silence came again, full of dark and evil portent. Boyd broke it this time. "Let's quit fooling around, Otis."

"Why would Tennant tell me?" Driscoll asked. "I was a stranger to him. I'd be the last person he'd tell."

"He must have told somebody," Hunter said. "He never told his wife, or her and the boy wouldn't be living the way they are. He never told any one else. The money's never been found, or Longstreet wouldn't still be looking for it. Come on, Driscoll, this is your one chance. Tell me where it is."

"I don't know," Driscoll said.

Hunter sighed. He gave a look at Boyd. "You were right, Frank. We've wasted enough time. Let's get started . . ."

They drove four stakes deep into the ground and then tied his wrists and ankles to them. He lay on his back with the merciless sun beating down on his face. He tried turning his head to one side and averting his eyes but the position was uncomfortable and he knew he could not hold it for long.

They stood one on either side of him, staring down as though proud of their handiwork. Hunter said, "We'll keep you alive, but if you're going to be stubborn you'll beg us to kill you. You'll get no food, no water, you'll stay just as you are until you tell us what we want to know. And don't bank on anyone stopping by to rescue you. Me and Frank are known as mighty unsociable people. Folks steer clear of Bar Cross Bar. When you're ready to talk just holler."

They went away then, leaving him alone.

He tried pulling on the thongs that bound him but all his efforts resulted in a cruel pinching of the rawhide about his wrists.

The sun bore down on him with increasing fury. It seemed that it gathered all its heat and focused it on him alone. He closed his eyes but the sun bored right through his eyelids. He kept turning his head, first to one side and then to the other.

After a while thirst began. The sun seemed to soak the last bit of moisture out of him and he began to dream of cool mountain springs and the shade of towering Ponderosa pines. Once he heard the running of water directly beneath him, only inches below the surface of the earth. Stop it, he told himself angrily, stop it right now or you're lost.

After an eternity the sun worked its way down toward the horizon. Not much longer, he thought. Soon it will be down. But would that avail him anything? I've got to get out of this, he said to himself. I've got to do something before I'm too weak. I can't wait until tomorrow. It's got to be done now.

What was that they had said? When you're ready to talk, just holler.

At first only a croak came from his mouth. After several attempts he began to get some sounds out. The efforts left him panting. He lay there, waiting for the jingle of spurs, the creak of leather boots. Then Hunter towered over him.

"Well, Driscoll?"

"Let me loose and I'll tell you."

Hunter smiled faintly and shook his head. "Tell us first."

"Can't you give me a little water? I can hardly talk."

"You'll get water after you've talked."

Driscoll swallowed and tried not to heed the sharp stabs of pain in his throat.

"In the Sombras, in a canyon."

Hunter's eyes took on a sharp, wary glitter. "Which canyon?"

"I don't know its name but I know where it is."

Hunter paused as though he were considering something. Finally he said, "All this is pretty vague. You realize that, don't you, Driscoll? You really haven't told us a damn thing."

"The Sombras have been searched," Boyd put in. "Nothing was found there."

"No one knew exactly where to look," Driscoll said. "But I do."

"Tell us, then."

"Like I said, I don't know the canyon's name but

I remember it. I used to hide the cattle I rustled in those mountains and so I know them. I remembered this canyon when Tennant told me about the rock with Indian painting on it."

Hunter turned and stared at Boyd. "I've heard of that canyon, Otis," Boyd said. "I've heard of that rock but damned if I know the way there. Nobody but some crazy prospectors have ever been there."

Hunter turned back to Driscoll. "All right, Driscoll, you better be telling the truth."

He felt his heart give a hard, swift thump when the thongs holding his wrists were severed by Boyd's knife. Then the thongs about his ankles were cut. He started to rise and then fell back, groaning. The two stared down at him as Driscoll rolled over on his knees and then rose slowly to his feet. They stood one on either side of him.

"Give me a drink, will you?" Driscoll said hoarsely.

"After we've got you tied on your horse," Hunter said. "Come on. Get moving."

Driscoll started ahead on tottering legs. He stumbled and almost went down. He felt Boyd grab for him and he leaned against the short man, clutching Boyd's right shoulder for support, and as his weight drove Boyd aside a short step Driscoll dropped his hand and grabbed at Boyd's pistol.

The short man let out a cry of alarm as he felt the weapon whipping out of his holster and he

38

made a futile reach for it. He started to whirl when Driscoll shot him with the barrel no more than an inch from Boyd's back. The cry choked in Boyd's throat and he began to collapse.

Driscoll knew that he could not hope to beat Hunter to the gun, but he came around fast and saw the black bore of Hunter's gun gaping at him and the harsh, feral gleam in Hunter's eyes.

It was greed that slowed Hunter. He wanted Driscoll alive, so he delayed a fraction of a second, searching for something other than a lethal spot, and in this tiniest of hesitations the bullet came whistling from out on the range, far to Driscoll's left, and slammed into Hunter's back.

The force of it drove Hunter ahead a step and as he wavered there, mouth gaping, a second slug hit him, smashing him to the ground. He fell without a moan, already dead before touching the earth.

The strange gun cracked again, this bullet crashing into Boyd, just struggling up. Boyd emitted a sharp, anguished cry and toppled over.

Driscoll was down flat on his stomach, wishing he had cover, pistol thrust out before him, searching the land for some sign of the hidden marksman. But only the grama showed, nodding sagely in the wind off the Sombras.

Then the voice came from behind a shed. "Davey, Davey, lad. Don't be so spooky. Put up that pistol. It's me, your friend and pardner—Lee Fairchild. Don't you remember me, Davey, lad?"

The beard gave Fairchild a haughty, crafty look. He had deepset eyes that gave the impression of watching slyly, secretly. He looked sleek and well-fed.

"You all right, Davey, lad?" Fairchild asked, thrusting his head forward to peer at Driscoll. "Those killers didn't hurt you, did they?"

"I'm all right," Driscoll said. He gave a glance at the two dead men, then looked back to Fairchild. "How come you got here when you did? I didn't even think you'd still be around. Aren't you taking a chance?"

Fairchild winked and grinned. "No one knows about me being your pardner in that rustling, thanks to you, Davey, lad. I knew you wouldn't squeal on me or Noel. It does my heart good to know I've been able to pay you back the favor."

"How did you know I was here at Bar Cross Bar?"

"I followed you out of Santa Loma. I didn't want to get in touch with you there for fear of what people might guess. Then these two killers jumped you and I trailed the three of you here. It made my heart sick to see you staked out there under that hot sun, Davey, lad. I was waiting for dark before I came to set you free."

"I'll bet," Driscoll said.

"What's that, Davey, lad? Don't you believe me? I didn't take the chance of trying to sneak in during daylight for fear that they might see me.

Not that I care what might happen to me—not when my pardner's life is concerned—but if they'd seen me and killed me, who would there have been to save you then?"

"All right, all right. Forget it."

"What they do a thing like this to you for, Davey?"

"They mistook me for someone else."

"It wouldn't have to do with that money Tennant stole, eh?"

"They thought I could tell them where it was. So I pretended I knew. I told them about the Indian rock canyon where we held those cattle once, and they fell for it. They'd have kept me staked there forever if I hadn't told them a good story."

Fairchild's eyes watched, probing, cunning. "But you *do* know where the money is, don't you?"

"No."

Fairchild's chuckle was soft and evil. "Come now, Davey, lad. You can trust your old pardner, can't you?"

"Get this straight, Lee. We're no longer pardners," Driscoll said. "I'm through with the old life. I don't owe you a thing."

"Don't you, Davey? What about these dead boys here? Hunter would have got you sure if I hadn't plugged him."

Driscoll frowned. This was the last man in the

world he wanted to be obligated to. He knew Lee Fairchild too well, knew him for a greedy and scheming and treacherous man.

"The only reason you killed Boyd and Hunter," Driscoll said, "was to get them out of the way. You don't give a damn what happens to me. You want me alive because you think I know where the money is. Doesn't that cancel any debt I might owe you?"

"Davey, lad," Fairchild said with horror, "how can you talk like that to me, your old pardner? We've rode many a dark trail together, we've shared food and blankets and shelter. How can you say things like that about me? You've hurt me, Davey."

"You can stop your play-acting, Lee," Driscoll said wearily, "because I don't know where Tennant hid his loot."

"Look, Davey. You were in jail with Tennant the last night he spent alive. He must have told you because no one has been able to find that money."

"If Tennant had told anyone, he'd have told his wife, wouldn't he?"

"She doesn't know."

"Is she still around?" Driscoll asked. "Has she married again?"

"She's around," Fairchild said, "and she hasn't got the money. Otherwise, she wouldn't be living as poorly as she is. But you sure know where

Tennant stashed his loot. Hell, you've got to know."

"I've had enough of you, Lee. Like I said, I don't feel beholden to you. Leave me be."

Fairchild reached out a hand, his fingers biting into Driscoll's biceps. "We shared everything when we were doing poorly. Now, it's not right or fair for you to get uppity, Davey."

Driscoll brushed the hand away. "I said leave me be."

"Thirty thousand, wasn't it, Davey? That's enough for two. You don't want to be a hog, do you, Davey, lad?"

"Lee. I don't know a damn thing about Tennant's loot."

"I won't be put off easy, Davey. Why do you think I stuck around? I knew you'd be back. That's what everyone in Santa Loma has been saying for over a year now. I got one of Longstreet's deputies drunk one night—not Hunter—that took Tennant from his cell when they hanged him, and this deputy told me how Tennant gave you a look before he was taken away. A lot can be said in one look, Davey."

Yes, Driscoll thought, a lot can be said in a look. Sorrow and thanks and a silent goodbye. I remember the look, too, and the boy's, full of pity because he'd been told the gallows was for me. I wonder how he felt when he learned it had really been for his father.

"There needn't be anyone else," Fairchild went on. "Just you and me. We don't have to cut Noel in at all."

"Noel?" Driscoll echoed. "Is he still around, too?" And he felt the bitterness in him deepen a little more.

"Sure. Didn't you know? He's working for Half Moon. But you know Noel. Give him a jug and he's happy. He's sweet on some girl, anyway, and that's all he's got on his mind now."

"You're just wasting your time, Lee," Driscoll said. "When Hunter and Boyd picked me up I was leaving Santa Loma for good. Soon as I get my horse I'll keep on."

"Then you've got it." Fairchild's voice was hoarse. "You're picking it up and riding away with it!"

"And what if I have?" Driscoll said angrily.

"You'll need me, Davey. You'll never get away with it by yourself. They'll be watching you, every move you make, everywhere you ride. Ain't Hunter and Boyd proof enough? But if you took me in with you, you could let me take the money while you decoyed them, and then we'd meet later and split. No one knows or suspects that we're pardners. You've got to take me in with you, Davey don't you see?"

"Ride on, Lee."

There was a pause. In the stillness Fairchild swore softly. "All right, Davey, lad, I'll go. But first let me tell you this: You'll rue this day and this hour. You'll rue the minute you kicked me out. They'll get you and they won't be gentle with you. When a slug is burning in your belly and you're dying with no one about to comfort you, you remember that you struck away my hand when I offered it to you in pardnership. Remember that with the last dying breath you take."

"Get, before I make you get."

Fairchild left with an angry jingling of his spurs. After a while there came the rising then fading sounds of running hoofs then there was nothing there at Bar Cross Bar but an echo of evil . . .

When he left Bar Cross Bar night was upon the land. He had dragged the bodies of Boyd and Hunter into a shed and left them there. Their deaths left him strangely unconcerned and unshaken, not at all like Tennant's death. He had never believed he could be so callous.

He slept that night under the stars and when morning came he headed westward toward the Sombras. He avoided high ground, and rode whenever he could in draws. He would ride up the mountain range and through the pass and down the western flank and that was the last the Sombras would ever see of him.

He had almost gained the foot of the pass when he spied the rider far behind him. He halted the black in the concealment of a cluster of large boulders and dismounted. He drew his pistol and checked the loads and began to wait.

When the black perked up its ears, Driscoll pressed his left hand across the horse's nostrils, stifling any whinny. Bit chains sang and a shod hoof rang against stone, then horse and rider hove into sight.

The rider made a quick, instinctive move toward his own gun. Then the hopelessness of it dawned on him and he stopped his hand scant inches from his pistol butt. He reined his bay in and his eyes rose and met Driscoll's.

Recognition came simultaneously. The two men's voices rang out together, calling one another's name.

Noel Reese was instantly out of the saddle, grinning as he stepped up to Driscoll. Suspicion, the aftermath of his stay in Santa Loma, cautioned Driscoll. He let the hammer of the pistol down but still held the gun.

Reese closed both hands about Driscoll's arms and squeezed affectionately. When Driscoll did not respond, the grin fled from Reese's mouth. His eyes dropped to the pistol that was almost jabbing him in the stomach.

"What the hell, Dave?" Reese said, lifting his eyes and staring puzzledly at Driscoll.

Shame came to Driscoll. He and Noel Reese had always been close friends. A weakness of the will and purpose was one of Noel Reese's faults, but duplicity had never been one of his vices. Lee Fairchild, Driscoll had never trusted. He had never doubted Reese's loyalty, however.

Driscoll put away his gun. His smile was bitter. "Sorry, Noel," he murmured. "I'm jumpy today."

Reese watched him gravely. "I'll say you're spooky, Dave. Did you think I was following you?"

"It sure looked like it."

"Why would I do a thing like that?"

Driscoll shrugged. He was thinking of Lee Fairchild and the cunning, hidden eyes of Santa Loma watching him.

Reese was staring at him closely. "I've never seen you so thin," Reese said, his voice oddly gentle. "Was the pen rough, Dave?"

"I lived through it."

"It was good of you not to squeal on Lee and me."

"Wouldn't you have done the same?"

"I might have but I don't think Lee would have." Blue eyes peered at Driscoll. "You see Lee?"

"I had a little talk with him yesterday." A thought occurred to Driscoll. "What's Lee do for a living now?"

Reese gave a soft, embarrassed laugh. "You never would play cards with Lee. Me, I never seemed to learn. We'd sell a few cows and I'd have a little money and take a few drinks and then Lee would riffle a deck of cards in front of me and

I'd be hooked. You always told me never to trust him and you were right. He always cleaned me."

Driscoll asked, "How does he get away with it?"

"Oh, Lee is good," Reese said ruefully. "He's got everybody fooled. He don't look or dress like a gambler. He goes around like a saddle-bum, dirty clothes and dirty hands. You know how clumsy he pretends to be when he shuffles but I'll bet he's the best seconds-dealer in the country. Then he doesn't win too much, just enough to get along. They've got him pegged as an easy-going, lazy gent in Santa Loma. No one gives him a second thought."

"You play cards with him any more?"

Reese showed a crooked smile. "Lee told me, right after you got sent up, that we better pretend we didn't know each other in Santa Loma. We don't cotton to each other any more. As for playing cards, I've given the pasteboards up, Dave. Drinking, too."

Driscoll could not free himself from the nagging suspicion. He seemed to have changed again, and his eyes beheld only deceit and conniving and trickery. They saw nothing that was frank and honest any more.

His voice was deceptively soft. "How come you and Lee stuck around here? I'd think the two of you would have beat it away from here after I got picked up and sentenced."

"I don't know about Lee," Reese said, voice

barely audible. "But, I found a good place to work and—" His glance rose, locked with Driscoll's in sudden defiance. "I like it here. I ain't done one thing against the law. I'm going straight now. Why shouldn't I stick around?"

Driscoll's gaze narrowed slightly. "And you weren't trailing me?"

"That's a crazy thing to accuse me of, Dave. Why, I didn't know it was you. I've been scouting for strays. I'm on my way back to Half Moon now. That's where I work. Why should anyone be trailing you?"

"You ever hear who was in jail with me in Santa Loma?"

"Jim Tennant," Reese said quietly. "Everybody remembers that."

"And you ask me why would anybody be trailing me?" Driscoll's voice was flat and hard.

"I've always passed that off as crazy talk, Dave," Reese said. His glance met and held Driscoll's.

A dim smile, without mirth, shadowed Driscoll's mouth. "What do *you* think, Noel?"

Reese made an impatient, irritated sound. "How the hell should I know? I never gave it a thought, one way or another."

The embittered smile curved Driscoll's mouth again.

"Look, Dave," Reese said, "I know what a lot of people began to think and say after Tennant had been hung and the money wasn't found, but not everyone sees it that way. Oh, there's been a lot of looking and searching and digging, but if anyone has found anything he hasn't said a word about it. There's been talk that maybe Tennant told his secret to you. But I never went along with that. Why would he tell *you?*"

"Thanks, Noel," Driscoll said dryly.

"If he told anyone he told his wife," Reese went on. "If anyone knows, she does, even if she lives in poverty. That's smart of her, the way I see it. Wait until it all dies down and then one night take the kid and the money and leave the country."

"It must be tough on her," Driscoll said quietly. "I mean going on living on the old place."

"Oh, she's not on their old place any more. They lost that but the bank in Santa Loma gave her another spread, a small one that no one wants— the old Quarter Circle Six, right next to Half Moon . . ."

The buildings of Half Moon looked drowsy and deserted in the late afternoon sun. Beyond them reared a barren, jagged peak of the Sombras, and as the two riders approached someone stepped out of the house and stood with hand-shaded eyes, watching them come on. The sun flashed coppery bright in red hair. It was a woman and she turned and went back in the house.

Noel Reese reined in near a corral in which two paints and a sorrel were standing, tails to the wind, and loosened his saddle cinches. Driscoll dismounted by the water tank. He loosened the cinches and then pulled the black's thirsty mouth out of the water and held the horse a moment. He heard Reese's shout as he opened the corral gate and hazed his bay inside.

A man came out of the house. The man was short and stocky with big, powerful shoulders and thinning sandy hair. His eyes met Driscoll's briefly. Then the man went on to Reese and stopped before him and spoke in a low tone.

The black had drunk his fill and Driscoll tightened the cinches. He had his left foot in the stirrup, ready to step up into the saddle, when the sound of Reese's approach deterred him. He stood as he was, boot in the stirrup, waiting.

"You're not leaving, Dave?" Reese said. "Stay and rest a while. It's all right with you, Mr. Duchaine, isn't it?"

The stocky man smiled. "I'd take it unkindly if you didn't, friend. I'm Fred Duchaine, and you're welcome to stay on at Half Moon as long as you wish. Noel tells me you're Driscoll."

He had just taken his foot from the stirrup and now he was sorry he had done so.

The smile died on Duchaine's face. He peered anxiously at Driscoll, sensing his bitter mood. "Did I say something wrong?"

"No," Driscoll said, and glanced to the south again. "Everything's all right, Duchaine."

"I took it for granted you'd stay for supper," Duchaine said. "My daughter's already working on it. She's fixing some for you, too." He laughed genially. "You see, we're just one family here at Half Moon, Driscoll. That right, Noel?"

"You bet. That's why I like it here, Dave." Reese grinned. "Rosalie's a damn good cook. I'll bet you ain't eaten anything as good since—" He caught himself then and flushed.

If Duchaine caught the unintentional inference he gave no indication. "Spend the night here, too, if you like, Driscoll. There's lots of room in the bunkhouse. You'll be company for Noel. Right, Noel?"

"I don't want to put you out," Driscoll said, looking to the south, in the direction Noel had told him Mrs. Tennant and her boy lived, on the Quarter Circle Six.

"No bother at all," Duchaine said. "Out of the way like we are here at Half Moon we get mighty few visitors."

Driscoll glanced once more to the south. Forget it, he told himself. Stay overnight and in the morning ride north. Leave for good.

"All right, Duchaine," he said.

He felt very uncomfortable, because this was something strange to him, eating at a table in a home, with china plates and cups instead of tin, without the somber dankness of prison or the guttering smoke of a lonely campfire stinging his eyes and wind blowing grit into his food. Something touched him deeply and he kept his eyes on his plate.

When the girl spoke he began to flush just at the sound of her voice. It had been so long since he had sat so close to a woman, just across the table from her, and she was young and very pretty. In the penitentiary he had forced himself not to think of women except one and her only because she did not stir him as other women did. To him she was just a memory, a worn, distraught face racked with anguish and sorrow. So it had been all right to think of her but not of anyone like Rosalie Duchaine.

"I'd think a man like you would eat much more than you have," the girl said. She had a soft, pleasant voice. It made him think of tiny silver bells.

"You could stand some fattening," she said, gentle banter in her tone. "My gracious. You're as skinny as a horse after a long, tough winter."

Then she must know about him and his prison record, as everyone in the county knew. Up to now what other people might think of that had not bothered him. At this moment, however, he cared very much.

Duchaine pushed his plate aside and sighed with satisfaction. "That's enough for me, too, Rosalie."

She flashed a wide, white smile. "You'll help me gather the dishes, won't you, Noel?"

He almost knocked his chair over as he rose to his feet. "Will you excuse us, Mr. Driscoll? Father will keep you company while I do the dishes."

Reese had a heap of dishes in his hands and went into the kitchen, followed by the girl. Their voices drifted into the parlor where Driscoll and Duchaine sat. The girl said something to Reese and laughed very softly. When Reese came out of the kitchen his face was flaming. He took his hat and said:

"Well, I'll go look after that colt now, Mr. Duchaine."

Duchaine nodded absently. He opened a humidor, took out two cigars and offered one to Driscoll. "Good boy," Duchaine said, nodding at the door through which Reese had gone. "A very good worker. I couldn't like him more if he was my own son. You two know each other long?"

Driscoll felt something tighten in his stomach. How much had Reese told about their past relationship?

"I met him up in Colorado," he said, which was the truth. "That was quite a few years ago. Then we drifted apart. I didn't see him again until today."

"That's what he tells me," Duchaine said, and relief washed through Driscoll. The man cocked his head to one side and for a few moments listened to the girl who was singing softly in the kitchen. "She's a fine girl, my Rosalie," Duchaine said, nodding in emphasis. "She's been both mother and daughter to me since my poor wife passed on. I'm proud of her."

Driscoll stared at the cigar in his hand and tried not to think of her, of the lissom movement of her long, slender legs. He felt the echo of a great loneliness, and he tried to think of another woman, of the distress and grief in her face, but these thoughts did not help at all.

"Are you just riding through, Driscoll?"

He came out of his somber reverie with a start. He took a puff on the cigar to cover his confusion. "That's right," he said through a cloud of tobacco smoke. "I had planned to be well up in the pass by nightfall but then I ran into Noel. I think I'll ride through the Sombras tomorrow."

"Driscoll," Duchaine said, "if you haven't got a job waiting for you someplace, I'd be glad to sign you on at Half Moon."

Pans clattered in the kitchen. The girl was humming now.

"Why?" Driscoll said at last, an ugly swirl of anger in him.

"I always add an extra man during the fall," Duchaine said, ignoring the sharpness of Driscoll's question. "This was a dry year and more cattle than usual have drifted up into the Sombras. Noel tells me we'll have quite a job rounding them up. I can always find someone but I feel you and

Noel, knowing each other, would get on together. The job's yours if you want it, Driscoll."

Bitterness came. "Don't you know what you'd be hiring?"

A pained look entered Duchaine's eyes and he glanced quickly away. "Driscoll, we all make mistakes. I did my share of helling around when I was young. What you did is your business. You paid for your mistake. The way I look at it, if everyone is going to hold that against you and not give you a break, you won't have any choice but to go back to what you'd been doing. I pride myself on being a good judge of character. That's why I'm offering you a job. If I had any doubts about you I would never do it."

"It isn't only that," Driscoll said, still sullen. "There's always Tennant."

There was utter silence now. No sounds came from the kitchen, but Driscoll could sense the girl's presence there. Duchaine expelled his breath audibly.

"Oh, yes—Tennant," Duchaine said quietly. His sigh was a weary wheeze. "You must have heard the talk about you and him and—" He broke off. "Hogwash! Just because the money has never turned up doesn't mean that someone hasn't got it. It stands to reason that anyone finding it wouldn't advertise the fact."

Duchaine leaned forward and emphasized his words now and then by moving the hand holding his cigar. "Only two people would have got the hiding place of that money from Tennant. His wife is the logical choice. Maybe she knows and is just biding her time, until she can get that money and be gone before any one can catch her. Only one other person would know." He paused, watching Driscoll. "That's Longstreet."

He saw the harsh look that came over Driscoll's face.

"You don't like him, Driscoll, do you?" Duchaine said. Without waiting for an answer, Duchaine went on, "I don't blame you. Longstreet's an out-and-out skunk if I ever saw one. You can understand why I say that if anyone got anything out of Tennant it was Longstreet. He could get water out of solid rock if he set his mind to it."

"I take it you don't like Longstreet, either."

Duchaine made a face and waved a hand. "Oh, he's never made me any trouble. I've never given him cause to. But I've never liked him and he knows it. I considered running against him once but then I figured if I ran and lost he'd get back at me. For myself I wouldn't care. But I've got Rosalie."

"How come he keeps getting elected?" Driscoll asked. "Everyone seems to hate him. Who votes for him, then?"

"Oh, he's got backing, strong backing. You see, this was a pretty wild country ten-fifteen years back. The big ranchers and the businessmen in

Santa Loma and Fort Britt got together and figured that only a killer could take care of the outlaws who were doing pretty much as they pleased. So they looked around and came up with Ira Longstreet."

Duchaine leaned back in his chair with a sour look on his face. "He'd been run out of Texas by the Rangers and he'd gone north and worked as a peace officer in Abilene and Ellsworth. They figured he was tough enough, mean enough to handle just about anything. He keeps law and order in the county. Sure, everyone knows what goes on in his jail but they say if a man keeps his nose clean he won't wind up in that jail. And Longstreet does keep law and order and his backers see to it that he keeps being re-elected. That's how it is, Driscoll."

"You figure then he knows where that money is?"

Duchaine said, "I'm just guessing and basing my conclusions on what I know about the man. I really haven't given that money much thought, Driscoll. I'm not one of these dreamers thinking that someday I'll stumble across a fortune that will make me rich for life. I stick to my ranch and live day to day. My girl is all I think about, all I work for." He peered at Driscoll. "You haven't told me yet your decision about that job."

"How about letting me sleep on it?" Driscoll said.

Duchaine smiled. "I like a man who's not too hasty with his decisions. That will be just fine, Driscoll . . ."

He grew restless and uneasy and by nightfall, in the bunkhouse, he had difficulty following Reese's chatter. The man sensed Driscoll's annoyance and became silent. His eyes followed Driscoll's pacing to the window and back.

All at once Driscoll could endure it no longer. It was the same feeling that had swept over him countless times in prison and he had clenched his teeth to keep from screaming. The sense of suffocation was overwhelming and now he could do something about it.

"I'm going out for some air," he told Reese.

Outside, the night was quiet except for the soft gusting of the wind. There was no moon but a myriad stars bored through the black sky and looked down on him like so many watching, curious eyes.

He found that he was looking south, where Quarter Circle Six lay, and he cursed himself under his breath. He knew what reason was telling him: Ride on, Driscoll, ride on. There's nothing here for you but trouble and maybe death. Be smart and ride on.

He tried arguing with himself. He had an offer of a job here. Duchaine impressed him as a sincere man. But still he could not get over the feeling of suspicion, of duplicity and treachery. It was a feeling that would be with him as long as he stayed on this range. It was like a malignant disease that he had contracted in the Santa Loma jail and which would eventually result in his own destruction.

He heard the soft steps behind him and his first instinct was to reach for his pistol but it came to him that his belt and gun were in the bunkhouse.

"Driscoll? Is that you?" the girl asked. She came ahead slowly, emerging from the shadows. Head cocked to one side, she peered at him.

"Is that you, Driscoll? I—I was startled."

"It's me." His voice was dry with resentment at her intrusion.

She wore a dark shawl over her shoulders and now she wrapped this tightly about her. For a while she stood there beside him, staring south as he had done. After a long time he could feel her eyes staring at him.

"Do you do this often, Driscoll? I mean, stand in the night and just look, with the wind on you and something in your heart you don't quite understand?"

He shrugged and harked to the grama rustling ever so softly against his boots. "I never paid much attention to how often I do it. I just seem to think better this way, that's all."

"I come out here almost every night," she said. "I can't quite explain it. The world seems so much bigger under the starlight. It makes me feel so small and alone but I rather like that feeling. Do you ever get lonely, Driscoll?"

He said nothing. Something cried briefly, anguishedly in him, then was still. The scent she was using drifted to his nostrils. All at once he became very much aware of her nearness. Then he thought of Duchaine and the pride and tenderness in his voice when he spoke of this girl. He forced his clenched fists open. He drove his glance back to the south where a woman lived that he had always associated with tears and sorrow.

She seemed unaware of what her presence was doing to him. Her voice echoed sweetness and innocence. "I get lonesome very often but this is a lonely country to begin with, and somehow I don't feel at home unless I am lonely with it." She gave a tiny, embarrassed laugh. "I don't suppose I make sense, do I, Driscoll? I suppose you think I'm crazy?"

"No," he said. "I guess that's how I feel, too, only I never was able to put it into words like you just did. I don't think I ever heard anyone put it better than you did."

"Thank you, Driscoll."

He saw her shudder. "Aren't you cold? That shawl isn't much protection against this wind."

"It *is* colder than I thought," she admitted. "Well, it's time I was getting back to the house, anyway. Father knows I come out here but he worries when I stay too long."

"Would you mind if I walked you to the house?"

"I'd like that very much, Driscoll."

As she came around, she lost her balance and he sensed her falling toward him and he reached out and caught her, steadying her. For a moment she was strong against him, and he felt his pulses pound. Then she was pulling away from him with a low, embarrassed laugh.

"How clumsy of me, Driscoll. I'm sorry."

He said nothing. He could only stand by, helpless and thwarted.

She started for the house and he walked beside her. He glanced at her once out of the corner of his eyes but she was looking primly down, hands and arms hugging the shawl to her body. For an instant a great longing cried in him and he yearned for comfort and the sense of belonging.

She mounted the porch steps and turned and looked down at him. "Thank you, Driscoll," she said. She paused. "I—I couldn't help overhearing earlier this evening. I mean, Father's offer of a job to you. Have you made up your mind?"

"I'll know by morning. I hadn't planned on staying around here."

"Oh. I'd hate to see you ride on. I mean, Noel has said so many nice things about you and Father thinks you'd be a good, reliable man. These drifters, you hardly ever can depend on them. I wish you'd consider Father's offer."

"I'll do that, Miss Duchaine."

In the darkness he could see the whiteness of her smile. "Good night then, Driscoll."

"Good night."

The door closed. He watched her shadow passing the lamplit window. Then he turned and started for the bunkshack.

CHAPTER 5

They all wore long faces. He shook Duchaine's hand and then Noel Reese's. To the girl he tipped his hat. An appeal swirled in her deep blue eyes, but his decision had been made. He would not veer from his resolution.

Duchaine said, "That job will always be open to you, son."

"Thanks, Duchaine."

Reese wore a glum expression. "I'd figured on having you around to jaw with for a while, Dave."

Driscoll's face was sober. His eyes told nothing.

"You know me, Noel," he said. "I've always got to see what's on the other side of the hill."

"You heading west?"

"South."

He saw them exchange looks and then stare at him with curious, intent expressions. He flushed a little. "I've always wanted to see the Border country," he said. "I might even try my luck in Mexico."

He could not tell if they believed him. Their expressions did not change. He thought the girl's lips tightened somewhat, as in disapproval. He touched the brim of his black hat and showed them a small smile. Reese lifted a hand in a half-hearted farewell. Duchaine and the girl made no sign at all.

The black responded eagerly to the touch of Driscoll's spurs.

Once he spied two riders far in the distance and it seemed to Driscoll that they were watching him from across the long, open space. But he could not discern who they were or what they were. Something raced uneasily down his spine and he loosened the pistol in its holster and then touched the stock of the rifle in the boot under his left leg.

He reached Quarter Circle Six near noon. Shadows were short and small. The wind was picking up again.

The grass grew sparser here. There was an air of meagerness, of hopelessness and futility about the land. There was an orphan atmosphere about not only the ground and vegetation but about the buildings as well, as though they merely existed, unwanted and forlorn.

There were several horses in one corral and two calves and their mothers in another. These were the only living things visible to Driscoll as he rode in. He pulled the black to a halt, dismounted and walked slowly around the yard, the black trailing him. The horses in the corral came over against the near side of the corral and in their milling one of them knocked a pole off the top of the corral fence. Driscoll went over, replaced the pole, then tested a post. He found the whole structure shaky.

The house was not much more than a shack. No smoke curled from the chimney and there seemed to be no one at home. Curtains hung in the windows. A few sad, wan flowers grew on either side of the front steps.

About the whole place there was an aura of something missing, a man's touch, his love and devotion for the land, for the structures he had built and, most of all, for people living in them.

A wagon stood to one side with one wheel off and the axle propped up on a couple of blocks of wood. A pail of grease lay near at hand but the axle itself was bone dry.

Driscoll went over to the bunkshack, leaving the black ground-hitched, and opened the door. The mustiness of the interior and the sounds of someone snoring struck him simultaneously. As he went inside, the sleeper snorted loudly and mumbled something, then the snores resumed, measured and untroubled.

The old man slept on his back in a bunk with one hand dangling within easy reach of a corked jug. Long white hair fanned out beneath his head.

Driscoll reached down and shook the man's shoulder. "Wake up, old-timer," Driscoll called. "Time to rise and shine."

The fellow almost choked on a snore. He sputtered and gasped and muttered, his bloodshot eyes turned slowly toward Driscoll at first with puzzlement and then sudden fear. The man came up on an elbow.

"Who—who are you? What you doing here? Who—where you come from?"

"Easy, old-timer," Driscoll said, looking about. A battered Henry rifle hung on pegs above the bunk. "I'm not going to hurt you. I just want to ask you some questions."

"I don't know nothing. There's no use asking me nothing. I'm just a sick old man." The fellow forced a cough. He peered at Driscoll with a new, quick fear. "You—you the law?"

"Don't you folks have enough law around here? I'd say Longstreet is more than enough law for anyone."

"You know Longstreet?" Fear panted in the old man's loud breathing. "Did he send you here?"

Driscoll felt himself tighten, every sense and intuition alert. His eyes narrowed as he watched the old man. "Why would Longstreet send me out here?"

The old man shrugged. His eyes took on a wary, veiled look. He sat up on the edge of the bunk now and reached down for the jug. As an explanation he forced another cough and rubbed his chest.

"I've been feeling poorly, mister," he said, and raised the jug and took two convulsive swallows. He shuddered and then wheezed. "A doc told me a sip now and then would help. There's no other medicine does me any good."

Something nagging and ominous was pawing at Driscoll's mind. It made him angry when he could not define it or discern its nature.

"What's your name, old-timer?"

"Montana. They call me that because I spent twenty years in the Bitter Roots. They were the best years of my life. I trapped and hunted and had me a Blackfoot squaw and some kids. But she died in a blizzard and I came south." He sniffled and wiped a tear from his eyes. "Prettiest place I ever seen, the Bitter Roots. I'd sure like to go there before I die."

"What you doing here?" Driscoll asked.

The contents of the jug were working in Montana. He squared his shoulders and became indignant. "I work here."

Driscoll thought of the wagon abandoned in the middle of greasing and laughed softly.

"I do, too," Montana said, bristling. Then his voice became a whine. "But I'm old and feeling poorly. I get the miseries in my back and chest every time I work too hard. I was greasing a wagon this morning when those miseries hit me real bad. I came in here for just one little nip—it's really medicine for me—and lay down for a couple of minutes and then you come and wake me up." He ended on a note of reproach.

"Who you working for?"

Montana's eyes blinked rapidly. "You mean here on Quarter Circle Six?"

"Where else?"

"Miz Tennant." The red-shot eyes were probing at Driscoll. "Ain't I seen you someplace before?"

Here it comes again, Driscoll thought darkly, and decided to ignore it. "Where is she? Mrs. Tennant?"

"What you want with her?"

"That's for me to tell her and no one else."

"I'm sure I seen you some place," Montana said, squinting.

"Never mind that," Driscoll growled. "Where's Mrs. Tennant?"

The voice said from the doorway, "Why do you want to know?"

Driscoll spun on a heel, hand whipping to his pistol. But she stood there in the doorway watching him without expression. Slightly behind her was the boy, also watching.

Driscoll slid the pistol back in its holster. Behind him he heard Montana move but paid him no heed until he heard Montana snarl: "All right, bucko. Put up your hands."

Driscoll knew sudden anger at himself for he had forgotten about the Henry rifle. He came around slowly and the Henry was pointed at his chest.

"Put that gun away, Montana," the woman said.

"Like hell I will," the old man snarled. "Don't you know who this is?"

Driscoll felt a chill run through him. He saw

the woman eye him closely, frowning, but no recognition came. The boy squeezed his way in alongside her and he stared with some glimmer of vague recollection.

"If he had intended harming you," the woman told Montana, "he would have already done so. Put that rifle down."

"Oh, no, Miz Tennant, not until I say my piece. This is Driscoll, Miz Tennant. The man who was in jail with your husband the night before he was hung."

Hazel Tennant's face grew ashen beneath the heavy tan. The brown eyes grew bright with tears. Her hand lifted to her mouth and she bit down hard on the knuckles, and it seemed that all the sorrow had returned to her face.

She disarmed Montana and invited Driscoll into the house. He sat uncomfortably on the edge of his chair while she started a fire and then put on the coffeepot. The boy sat on the far side of the room, playing with a belt and holster and a sixshooter.

"I wish you wouldn't play with that pistol, Billy," the woman said wearily.

"It's not loaded," the boy said. "I made sure of that."

"That's not the idea. I just don't like you playing with guns, even if they're empty. Can't you find something else?"

The boy pouted. "It's mine. Pa gave me this

pistol. It was his but he gave it to me and it's all mine. It's the only thing I got to remember him by."

A look of pain crossed the woman's face and she bit her lip. She was wearing a man's red and white checkered flannel shirt and faded and patched Levi's. All the work in the saddle would have to be done by her, with what little help the boy could give. Montana? He was of no use anywhere, Driscoll thought, and wondered about that.

She was a year or two younger than he, Driscoll figured, but a strand or two of white already showed in her dark hair. Her face, although haunted by torment and desolation, still carried a hint of prettiness.

The coffee was warm. She poured a cup for Driscoll and one for herself. The boy kept cocking the pistol and snapping the trigger.

"You're going to ruin the spring that way, Billy."

"Aw, Ma. I can't do nothing any more."

She sighed wearily and looked at Driscoll. Her eyes were clear now and direct. "Well, Driscoll, what do you want to see me about?"

He shifted in the chair and took another sip from his cup. Until now it had been quite simple in his thinking: He would find out where she lived and look her up and help her if she needed help. He had never considered putting it into words.

He folded a hand about his cup and stared down into it, seeing everything all different now,

71

everything changed and difficult, not at all as he had used to envision it.

"You know what I am, what I've been," he said in a low voice. "I need work. I thought you might be able to hire me."

When he looked up she was watching him with a small, strange smile. The instant he saw the wary glitter in her eyes he knew there was no mirth there.

"Why?"

The bluntness of the question set him back. This was not a broken woman here. There was still steel in her.

He gestured. "The way the place looks— Montana isn't much use. Do you have another hand?"

She shook her head. She was watching him with grim amusement, her attitude telling him he was not fooling her.

A woman watching him like this—he did not know how to cope with it. "Well?" he said, exasperated because she flustered him. "How about it?"

"Have you tried to get a job elsewhere?"

He decided to lie. "Yes," he said. "No luck."

"Did they tell you why, give you any reason?"

He might as well go along with the lie. "Only that they were full up and didn't need any more riders."

"What places did you try?"

He felt warmth start for his face and he silently cursed himself. Why had he tried to lie when he knew he'd always made a very poor liar? Anger broke out in his voice though she could not understand the true reason for it.

"Do we have to go through all this?" he growled. "Do I get a job or don't I?"

She dropped her glance to the table and he breathed a sigh of relief. "Isn't it strange, Mr. Driscoll," she said, still looking down, "that you should have come back here to seek work after—after having been away? Wouldn't it have been less embarrassing for you if you'd gone some place where you and your past were both unknown? Not only less embarrassing, but giving you a much better chance of finding employment. Isn't that right?"

Her glance rose suddenly and locked with his. It pinned him where he sat. She might have known grief and anguish and despair but she was not vanquished. Despite the aura of brooding and anxiety and fear that hovered over Quarter Circle Six, she was not as helpless, as bewildered, as he had always imagined her to be.

He decided to abandon deceit and be forthright and honest. "I just want to help you," he said quietly.

"Why?"

Again the one word. And he could not answer. The words were there in his heart but how was he to voice them? Should he tell her that it was only remembrance of her and the boy that at times had preserved his sanity? He feared if he told her that she would laugh at him. So he said nothing.

At last the woman sighed. "I'm sorry, Driscoll. I have no need for you or any one else. I have all the help I need."

He looked at her now. For the first time her glance wavered from him to the window.

"You know that's not true," he said quietly. "There's a lot that needs repairing. The fall roundup will be coming on. Old Montana's no good for anything like that. You can't kid me, Mrs. Tennant. He's a drunk and nothing else."

Her lips paled and tightened. She still did not look at him. "Are you trying to tell me how to run my ranch, Driscoll?"

"I'm just stating facts. Montana's passed his usefulness. You need a man who can do a full day's work."

She gazed at him with that strange smile. "I know all about Montana, Driscoll. I am very well aware of all his failings. I keep him on because he's the only hand I can afford. All he asks for is something to eat and a place to sleep. I pay him no wages at all because I can't afford to pay wages. Now do you understand, Driscoll?" Her voice broke slightly. "I still have a little pride left."

He had not reckoned on anything at all like this. With the innocence of a child he had dreamed of riding up and offering his services and magically setting everything in order.

"I'll work without pay," he said, and then quickly amended it. "Until you've sold some cattle and can pay me."

For the first time he saw anger in the brown eyes. The hand on the table closed into a fist.

"It's not natural for anyone to work for nothing," she said stiffly. "Not anyone as young and able as you. So you must have another reason for wanting to stay on. What is it?"

He could not tell her the truth, the feeling in his heart, for she would not believe him. After all, she knew nothing about him that would cause her to trust him. So he said nothing.

"Are you after the money?"

That brought his glance up sharply. Anger and hostility showed in her eyes.

"Are you going to pretend you don't know what I mean?"

Dully, sadly, he shook his head. Now he knew definitely that it had been a mistake for him to come back.

"I think we understand each other, then. Will you leave now, Driscoll?"

He did not know what prompted him to make one last try. "I really don't care about the money. Honest. I just—"

He saw the unbelieving look in her eyes and that silenced him. She rose to her feet.

"I'll thank you to leave immediately, Driscoll."

"You better do what my Ma says."

The click of the pistol being cocked brought Driscoll twisting around sharply in the chair and he found himself staring into the bore of the six-shooter. The boy held it with both hands but the weapon was steady and aimed at Driscoll's chest.

The woman drew in her breath in a sharp, startled inhalation.

"Don't you think I don't know how to shoot," the boy said, glaring at Driscoll. "This gun is loaded now. You just look. And you better leave pronto or I'll blow your head off!"

CHAPTER 6

From a distance he watched Reese ride down to the water hole and dismount. Reese loosened the cinches and then let the bay drink. When he was sure that Reese was alone, Driscoll mounted the black and rode up out of the draw. Reese saw him coming, his face sober as Driscoll rode up. Reese nodded.

There was an air of reluctance about both men. Driscoll became instantly aware of this. It was like a wall around them, sealing one off from the other. Driscoll built a smoke and then offered the makin's to Reese who accepted and rolled a cigarette without saying a word.

Reese broke the silence. "I thought you were riding south."

"I changed my mind."

Reese held his cigarette up and stared at it as though it held something that interested him. "How far did you get—before you changed your mind?"

Driscoll no longer cared who knew or what they might think of him. Perhaps his mistake had been in pretending to be something he was not, in not playing it right across the boards.

"Quarter Circle Six."

Reese stared down at the dirty water, muddied by the white-faces, two of which were standing in it. "Oh?" was all that Reese said.

"What's going on there?"

Reese peered at him. "What you mean?"

"Something's going on and it has to do with that money Tennant stole and hid. That woman puts on a brave front, but she's scared to death of something. You can feel it all over the place."

"What did you go there for?"

"To help her and the boy," Driscoll said. His eyes dared Reese to challenge that. "The first time in my life I ever saw her and the boy was when they came to the jail to say goodbye to Tennant. I promised myself then that if I could ever do anything for them I would. They're in trouble now and I aim to help them. You know what it's all about. Tell me."

Reese sighed, a long, weary sound. "Forget it, Dave. You can't win. Either ride to the Border or head across the Sombras. Forget the Tennants, forget this range. It's the only thing you can do."

"What if I can't forget?"

Reese stared at him with a long, sharp look. "Wasn't once enough for you?" he asked quietly. "You want to end up in that Santa Loma jail again?"

"Longstreet!" The word burst out of Driscoll harshly, venomously. He was surprised that he had not deduced this himself. It had to be Longstreet.

No one else could intimidate and terrify to such an extent. "He's the one behind it all, isn't he?"

He sensed Reese's cautious withdrawal. "You can't buck Longstreet, Dave. Don't try."

"What's the setup?"

"Let it be. It's no skin off your nose."

"I want you to tell me, Noel."

Reese stared at him wonderingly. Then he shrugged and looked away. "All right. If you're tired of freedom, even of living. Only old Montana Parker works for Quarter Circle Six because he's a drunk and good for nothing else. Oh, Hazel Tennant's tried hiring other riders but something always happens to them. Somehow they get drunk and disorderly the first time they go to town and Longstreet has to throw them in his jail and give them a good going over. Anyway, that's what he says. As for the riders, they just saddle up and ride away. No one ever sees hide or hair of them again."

Driscoll began to experience a strange eagerness. "Does Longstreet ever call at Quarter Circle Six?"

"What you mean by that?"

This time Driscoll's snarl was evident. "Is he courting her?"

He saw the look of disapproval that crossed Reese's face. "After all, Dave, Longstreet hung her husband."

"You think that would faze him? You think anything would? Now answer my question."

Reese kicked at the ground. "He does go there now and then, but what's to stop him? They say that Mrs. Tennant is afraid of him. But he's the sheriff and it's his job."

"Has it ever occurred to you that Longstreet is after that money, too?"

"Sure. He makes no bones about it. It's his job to recover it if he can."

Driscoll laughed harshly. "What kind of men do you have in this county, anyway, to let anyone terrorize a woman the way Longstreet is doing?"

"What the hell, Dave? Don't forget Tennant was a bank robber and a murderer. That money was stolen. I feel sorry for Mrs. Tennant, too, but if she knows where that money is and tries to get away with it, she's breaking the law."

Contrition came quickly to Driscoll. "I'm sorry, Noel."

"That's all right, Dave. I don't blame you."

"If you could have seen her that time, her and the boy. And Tennant, too. He wasn't a bad sort. Oh, he did wrong and deserved what he got. He never denied that or cried about it. He just cried for his wife and kid. I don't think I can ever—" All at once he couldn't finish.

"I know, Dave. I understand. But it's no good. You'll be bucking the whole business all by yourself. There won't be one person to stick up for you or give you a hand."

Driscoll thought, I know I'll be all alone. Not even her or the boy will be on my side though I'll be fighting for them. No one believes me, no one trusts me. But I've got to do it.

"Well, thanks for the information, Noel," Driscoll said. He picked up the black's reins.

"Where you going?"

"I don't know."

"How about coming to Half Moon? You'll be welcome there. You know what Duchaine told you."

"I want to be alone. I've got some deep thinking to do." He stepped up on the black.

Reese said, "Will I be seeing you again?"

A recklessness which he had not known in a long time brought a grin to Driscoll's face. "If you don't, just look for me in Santa Loma. I'll probably be in Longstreet's jail."

Reese grinned also but he could not conceal his anxiety and doubt. "Okay, Dave. I'll do that."

Driscoll brushed the black with the spurs and the horse broke into a run.

From high ground far away, he watched the buildings of Quarter Circle Six until nightfall came and he could see them no more. Then he mounted and rode on, heading westward toward the Sombras.

He came at last to a creek where a grove of junipers sheltered him and the black from the chill gusts off the Sombras. He unsaddled the black and picketed it and then set about building a fire.

He ate a lonely meal and then washed the tin plate and cup and the frying pan and coffeepot in the brook. The wind carried the shrill crying of a coyote.

He carried his blankets and his saddle just beyond the reach of the firelight and unrolled the blankets there and lay down on them, using the saddle as a pillow.

He put his belt and holstered pistol close to his hand and also placed within easy reach his Winchester. Then he tried to sleep.

He heard the faint gurgling of the brook and the restless stirring and pacing of the black who had never been this nervous since Driscoll had had him. He heard the urgent whisper of the wind as it sought to tell him its numberless secrets and once a scurrying nearby as of some tiny night prowler hurrying past.

Driscoll had no idea what it was that warned him. All at once it was there in him, the feeling that somewhere in the dark something was stalking him. It could be a trick of a tense imagination, but he grabbed his pistol and Winchester, removed his spurs, and moved quietly away into the junipers.

The black whinnied loudly. Was there an answer to the black? Driscoll strained his ears. There had been something out there somewhere in the night, perhaps a challenging neigh.

He moved on, in the direction of that phantom neigh, walking as quietly as he could, the pistol which he had thrust into his waistband rubbing against his middle, the rifle growing moist in his grip.

The trees thinned and opened on a small clearing. He sensed the movement at first rather than saw it. A darker, denser shadow than the others, a furtive stealing along the far side of the clearing. Black wrath raged in Driscoll. He laid the first slug just in front of that ghostly movement. Gun flame was a long, orange lance severing the night. On the heels of the crack of his rifle there came a startled cry.

The shadow darted back into the junipers and he followed it with another bullet, not caring whether this one hit or missed. Something flashed in the trees across the way and a slug whistled past his ear. He dropped swiftly to the ground and, flat on his belly, sprayed the junipers with bullets. When the rifle was empty he took the pistol in his hand and lay there, waiting for the echoes to die and silence to come.

The only sounds he heard after that was a frantic hurrying of hoofbeats that quickly faded and vanished. He lay there a long time, sweating in the cold night, his heart beating strong and loud against the earth . . .

• • •

The land was washed in sunlight when he awoke. He thought how different it looked, how clean and innocent, without the shadows of night blanketing it and terror hunting and prowling in the darkness. It almost looked like a good place to live in.

He ate and after that saddled the black and rode in the direction of Quarter Circle Six. The boy was in the yard and saw him coming. The boy ran into the house and quickly came out again, followed by his mother. She stood there with the boy close to her, one hand on his shoulder, hair stirring gently in the breeze, watching as Driscoll rode up.

He looked about but saw no sign of Montana. The bunkshack door was closed. When he brought his glance back to the woman he saw that she was staring at him with coldness and hostility. Driscoll stepped down from the black.

He said, "I'm here to help you, nothing more. You aren't driving me away this time. I have a good reason for wanting to help you and it has nothing to do with that money from the Fort Britt bank. Whoever's got it, what they do with it, doesn't interest me. I don't expect you to be civil to me or even talk to me, but there's a lot to be done around here and I aim to do it. When it's done I'll ride away and you'll never see me again."

A spasm crossed the woman's face. The

directness of her stare faltered, her eyes grew bright. Driscoll saw her hand close tightly about the boy's shoulder. Her son glanced at her with a twinge of pain twisting his face and a querying look in his eyes.

"Please," she whispered. "I appreciate what you mean to do, but I don't want to be responsible for anything happening to you."

Driscoll showed her a small, wry grin. "Just about everything that can happen has already hit me. Don't you fret about me, Mrs. Tennant."

"You don't understand." She still spoke in a strained, frightened whisper. "I don't know how to tell you."

"I know," he said, and was very grim all of a sudden. "I know how things stand here. I can take care of myself, Mrs. Tennant. I've twisted the tiger's tail more than once and I'm still around."

"I won't be able to pay you."

He looked right through her. "I'll put my bedroll in the bunkshack," he said, and started to lead the black away . . .

There was no one in the bunkshack and the place was none too clean. Driscoll told himself he would sweep it out and put it in order that evening or make Montana do it.

He unsaddled the black then turned it into the corral. The wagon still stood with one wheel off. He greased the wagon, replaced the wheel, and then set about strengthening the corrals. The work washed him with sweat but he relished the feeling. When sundown came he washed up at the tank by the windmill. There was still no sign of Montana and Driscoll began to hope that the old man had left Quarter Circle Six.

He cleaned the bunkshack and then decided he would cook himself something in the open. He got the coffeepot and frying pan and some beans and fatback and started for the door.

The woman had come out only a couple of times. Once she had puttered for a while among the few sorry flowers but he had never caught her glance on him. The boy had played in the yard but had kept his distance. Once Driscoll caught the boy watching him solemnly and Driscoll had smiled. The boy had turned and gone around behind the house.

So Driscoll was surprised when he stepped outside and found the boy approaching. He was carrying a large platter heaped with food and he walked with careful deliberation so as not to spill anything. A quick smile came to Driscoll and then something else, something that put a lump in his chest and stung his eyes. The boy became aware of Driscoll now and the lad stopped and raised grave eyes to Driscoll.

"Ma said to bring you this."

Driscoll set his things on the step and bent and took the platter from the boy. "Thank you, Billy," he said.

"Ma said if that isn't enough, she's got more. Just holler."

Driscoll looked down at the steak and potatoes and gravy and corn and a slab of pie.

"I've got plenty here," he said. "Your Ma shouldn't have put herself out like this."

"Ma always fixes a plate for Montana. Sometimes, though, he don't eat much, nothing at all."

"Where is Montana? I haven't seen him."

"He went to Santa Loma this morning. Said he had to get medicine or something."

Driscoll sat down on the bench in front of the bunkshack. "You want a piece of steak, Billy? It sure looks good."

"Naw. I ate already."

"You want to sit here by me then while I eat?"

The boy shifted uneasily. "I got to go help Ma." He started off, and presently the door slammed and the boy was gone.

He heard the horse coming in the darkness and his first impulse was to douse the lantern and grab a gun. Then he told himself not to be so edgy. The horse was approaching quite openly. There was no stealth or wariness in the sounds it made.

The horse passed the bunkshack and moved on to the corrals. Driscoll peered out the window and saw that it was old Montana, stripping bridle and saddle from his mount.

Montana pulled up sharply and hugged the jug

tightly against his chest as though he held some precious child which he sought to shelter and comfort. His red-shot eyes blinked rapidly at Driscoll. The odor of corn whiskey traveled across the room.

"What you doing here?" Montana's voice was baleful.

"I'm living here now, Montana. We're pardners."

"Pardners?" Montana repeated the word fuzzily. He stood clutching the jug. "You got no business here. Get out."

"I'm sorry, Montana," Driscoll said softly, "but I *do* have business here. I work here now."

"Work?" The red-veined eyes batted angrily. "You ain't fooling me. Didn't Miz Tennant run you off the place yesterday?"

"That's right. But that was yesterday."

The red-stained eyes stilled now. They studied Driscoll with a sly, intent watchfulness. "What did you tell her to talk her into letting you stay here?"

Caution came to Driscoll. He took another look at Montana. The man was old but there was a cunning about him, an air of duplicity and treachery.

"I just told her I was staying until the jobs that had to be done were done. You know the jobs I mean, Montana."

The old man stirred now. He went over to his bunk and carefully placed the jug on his blankets.

He sat down and slowly, gruntingly worked off his boots. He stared down at his stockinged feet and wiggled his toes.

"I ain't well," he said, looking at Driscoll. "I do the best I can. It's just that I ain't so young no more. I get the miseries, in my back and in my chest." He intercepted Driscoll's look at the jug and Montana's tone became indignant. "This here is medicine for me," he said, laying a caressing hand on the jug. "I got doctor's orders to take a nip now and then. It helps the blood circulate. If you don't believe me, go ask Doc Hartwell."

"I'll do that next time I'm in town."

"You ain't so smart," Montana said with a sneer. He sniffled. "I've seen smart young fellers like you come along, but they don't last long."

A strange excitement stirred in Driscoll. "How come?" he asked quietly.

Montana's old eyes glittered with wicked amusement. "I'm gonna let you find out all for yourself. *He-he-he.*"

"How come *you* last on at Quarter Circle Six?"

Montana peered warily at Driscoll. "I ain't so useless as you might think. As soon as I get over this attack of the miseries I'll make up my work. Miz Tennant knows that. That's why she keeps me on. Miz Tennant's a good woman. There ain't a thing I wouldn't do for her," he said virtuously.

"I'm glad to hear that," Driscoll said dryly. "Is that why you've let everything go to pot?"

The old man bristled. "Now look here, Driscoll, you mind your tongue. One word from me and—" He broke off abruptly and sat, staring balefully at Driscoll.

"And what?" Driscoll prodded softly.

"Never mind what. You'll find out." A titter shook Montana's shoulders. "You damn right you'll find out. *He-he-he.*"

"What if I make you tell me?"

Montana shrank back on his blankets. His eyes sought the Henry rifle on the pegs above his bunk, then swung back to Driscoll. "I didn't mean nothing," he whined. "I'm an old man. My mind don't work so good sometimes. I say things I don't even know I'm saying. I didn't mean nothing, Driscoll."

That restlessness was prodding Driscoll again. He told himself that Montana was old; so, not trusting himself, Driscoll went outside.

Lamplight glowed in a window of the house and Driscoll paused and stared at it. He walked slowly over to the corrals and the black noticed him and came to the bars with a lonesome, plaintive nicker. He stroked the black's muzzle absently; his thoughts were far away . . .

Montana had been working on the jug. His eyes had a bright, happy glaze. He was staring into space but the moment Driscoll entered the bunkshack, Montana blinked twice, then focused his gaze on Driscoll.

"You really must be sick," Driscoll said, "seeing how much medicine you have to take."

Montana remembered to cough. "It ain't that I like to drink. Honest, Driscoll. I hate the stuff." He made an unconvincing face. "But it's the only thing that picks me up. I tell you I get the miseries real bad. Any man but me would be moaning all the time. But I'm real tough. Don't forget I lived among the Blackfeet. Had me a Blackfoot squaw, I did, and some kids. Don't know what happened to them. Haven't cared about anything since." Tears gathered in the red-rimmed eyes.

Driscoll sat down on his bunk and pulled off his boots. He sat there, absently scratching his side and watching Montana. The old man's head dropped. He sniffled once and mumbled to himself, then lifted the jug and took a prodigious swallow.

He set the jug down with great care and solemnly corked it. "Want a drink, Driscoll?"

Driscoll shook his head.

"Come on. Have one." Montana lifted the jug.

"No, thanks, Montana."

"I know I should've offered you a drink right off. But my mind don't work so good no more. I get all mixed up. I forget things. I don't know what I say. You don't have to drink out of the jug. I'll get you a cup."

"Don't bother," Driscoll said. "I don't want any."

It was as though Montana had not heard. He rose to his feet, reeled sideways a step, then caught his balance. He went over to a shelf in a corner and came back with a tin cup. He set the cup carefully on the table in the center of the bunkshack, burped once loudly, and then poured. When the cup sloshed over he stepped back and waved a hand grandly.

"There you are, Driscoll. Have a little snort on me."

"I told you I didn't want any," Driscoll said. He removed his shirt and lay down on his blankets.

Montana made a hurt sound and mumbled something to himself. He made his way with effort to his bunk and sat down. This time he set the jug on the floor and then stared gravely across the room at Driscoll.

"Why don't you like me, Driscoll?"

Irritation stirred in Driscoll. "I never said I didn't."

"I know. I can tell."

"Go to sleep, Montana. Forget that jug."

"Oh, I don't need no more medicine now. I just want to talk. I want to be friends with you."

"All right, Montana. We're friends."

Montana stared at him. Tears formed in the old man's eyes. "You don't mean it. You're just saying it to make me shut up. I can tell when a man means what he says."

Driscoll said nothing.

"I'm just a poor, sick, old man," Montana said. He sounded on the verge of blubbering. "I ain't had much luck. Everything I tried went against me. The only happy days I knew were the years I spent in the Bitter Roots. That's where I want to be buried. I got sons there, if I can find them. Maybe they'll look after me and bury me. But I got no money to get there, Driscoll. All I need is just enough money to take a train there. It wouldn't be much. You could spare it, Driscoll."

Driscoll felt the tightness come, like a constricting band closing powerfully about his stomach. He told himself this was what he would have to put up with as long as he stayed on this range. No one was forcing him to stay. On the contrary, most people kept warning him to leave. So he clenched his teeth and stared at the ceiling.

"I know," Montana said, with drunken slyness. "I can tell you know where that money is. Maybe it's right here on this ranch. Is that why you're staying here, Driscoll?"

"Oh, shut up, Montana. Even if I did know I wouldn't tell you. You realize that, don't you?"

"I'm not trying to get you to tell me where it is, Driscoll. I just want enough to get to Montana. Just a few dollars. Won't you give me that much, Driscoll? Please?"

"Shut up and go to sleep."

The old man lifted supplicating hands while the tears trickled into the soiled whiskers. "I ain't got much farther to go. I can feel the grave reaching for me. Please, Driscoll?"

With an angry sound Driscoll got out of his bunk and went over and blew out the lantern. The darkness seemed to magnify the old man's weeping as his pleading went on.

Driscoll lay on his back, staring up at the shadows, then heard a gurgle as Montana drank from the jug again. He sobbed a few more times, then he began to snore.

All that night Driscoll kept dropping off and then coming awake abruptly, on edge and listening. Driscoll kept remembering the Henry rifle above Montana's bed and the greed in the crying, sniveling voice. Driscoll kept his pistol near at hand.

When morning came Driscoll felt worn and beaten and more exhausted than the evening before. Montana still slept.

CHAPTER 7

The boy brought a pot of coffee and flapjacks for breakfast. Then he hurried away. There was enough food for Montana, also, but Driscoll let the old man sleep. He wanted no repetition of the tears and whining of the night before.

He went to the corrals and saddled the black, mounted and rode close to the house purposely but no one appeared, not even the boy. The gay curtains in the windows were the only signs of occupancy.

He struck out across the land, heading westward toward the Sombras. He knew it looked as if he was leaving but the woman had only to check the bunkhouse. She would find Driscoll's blankets still there, an indication that he planned on returning.

He would have liked to take the boy with him, for company and also to have the boy point out the boundaries of Quarter Circle Six. There were no fences here. He could not tell where one ranch ended and another began. The only barrier was the rugged range of the Sombras to the west. Cattle drifted there and were easily lost in the desolate, forsaken canyons. Three years back he had helped quite a few cows lose themselves there.

He ranged the red hills here at the foot of the mountains and came upon several bunches of cattle. They were mostly Quarter Circle Six cows with some Half Moon and a Diamond K brand and a Running M. The calf crop seemed fair for fall. He noticed several large calves weaned from their mothers and no longer following them. These were mavericks with no sign of ownership burned on their hides and thus would belong to the first person to brand them.

He roped two of these calves and then built a small fire and heated his running iron until the hooked end was red hot. Then he went over to the two calves tied on the ground and burned the Quarter Circle Six brand on each one. He was about to release them when the black whinnied sharply.

He dropped the running iron and whipped around, pulling at his pistol. He had it almost out of the holster when the voice cracked down at him from a cottonwood grove nearby.

"Hold it, Driscoll."

He went rigid. Hate began to fan through him but he was helpless. There was nothing he could do but release the pistol and raise his hands.

The sun flashed brightly off the badge on Longstreet's shirt. He wore a wide grin as he came down the slope with gun leveled and spurs clanking. He glanced from Driscoll to the two bound, freshly branded calves.

"Back to your old tricks, hey, boy?"

Driscoll said nothing.

"This time I'll see that you get it good," Longstreet said. "I'll see that they put you away for as long as they can. I warned you not to make me put you in my jail again."

"Look at the brands," Driscoll said.

It was as though Longstreet had not heard him. Longstreet's grin was savage, brutal. "I don't think I'll wait until I get you in my jail, Driscoll. I think I'll start on you right now. It'll be a good lesson for any one else with ideas like yours to see you riding into Santa Loma looking real rough. Drop your gunbelt, boy."

"I said look at the brands," Driscoll said.

"And I said drop your gunbelt." Longstreet spoke softly.

"Look at those heifers, then," Driscoll said. "They're mavericks. I could have put any brand I wanted on them and there isn't a damn thing you can do about it. Look at them, Longstreet."

Longstreet's pale eyes flickered but the brutal purpose in him still held. "You resisting me, boy?" he purred.

"If you'd look at the brands," Driscoll said, "you'd see that they're Quarter Circle Six."

The grin died on Longstreet's face. A darkness passed over his features. Then, raging eyes still fixed on Driscoll, he started circling the bound calves until they were between him and Driscoll.

Only then did Longstreet's eyes dip down, then up again swiftly.

Disappointment filled Longstreet with wrath. Then the sixshooter slid back into his holster.

"That's right. You're working for Quarter Circle Six now, aren't you, boy?"

"You knew that before you threw a gun on me, didn't you?" Driscoll said, lowering his hands. The glitter in Longstreet's eyes dared him to reach for his pistol. The man was all on edge, aching to provoke Driscoll.

"That's right, boy."

"How'd you find out?"

"It's my business to know everything that goes on in my county."

"Did you spy on me?" Driscoll asked. He had a searing remembrance of two nights ago and those distant, ghostly hoofbeats drumming briefly in the night. "Is that how you found out?"

Longstreet gave his jarring laugh. "Spy? How can anyone spy on a thief and ex-convict? That's not spying. That's being careful. Now what I want to know is—what did you tell Miz Tennant to get her to hire you? She'd never hire a thief and ex-con."

Driscoll took a deep breath. "I didn't tell her anything. She just needs the help. Anyone can see that."

Longstreet's pale eyes glittered, jeering, challenging. "The only person you're interested in helping," Longstreet said with a sneer, "is yourself."

"You think the reason I want to hang around Quarter Circle Six is because I know where the money is that Tennant stole in Fort Britt. Isn't that right, Longstreet?"

Longstreet was a while in answering. Wariness came to him, an animal vigilance and caution.

"No," he said at last, "it's not quite that way, Driscoll. I don't believe you know where the money is. I might be wrong, but I don't think so. Tennant stole that money for his wife and kid. He wasn't going to hand it over to a stranger he'd just met. It's not quite like you said it is, Driscoll."

"Then how is it?"

The yellow eyes probed and examined. Longstreet said, "The logical thing for you to have done when you got out of the pen was to ride some place where you weren't known. Yet you came back. And I know why."

Driscoll smiled without mirth. "That money? But you just said you don't think I know where it is."

"Someone knows," Longstreet said darkly. "Tennant told someone and that someone has to be his wife. Now do you know why I'm calling you a rotten, sneaking, greedy snake?"

He's trying to find out if I heard him and Tennant that night, Driscoll thought, and knew a savage pleasure. He doesn't know for sure, and that's one satisfaction I won't give him.

"I've heard tell that you're more anxious than anyone to get your hands on that money."

"Why the hell shouldn't I be?" Longstreet exploded. "It's my job as sheriff isn't it? A bank failed and two good men died because of that damn money. Why shouldn't I try to recover it?"

"I'm glad to hear you talk like this," Driscoll said wryly. "The law is in good hands in this county."

The yellow eyes pondered and something wicked glittered in their depths. "You know, Driscoll, you stick around this range and you'll find yourself in more trouble than you've bargained for. You ever visit Bar Cross Bar?"

Driscoll felt a cold knot in his stomach. "Bar Cross Bar?" he repeated as calmly as he could. "I only remember the brand from three years back."

"The place is run by Otis Hunter and Frank Boyd. Yesterday somebody found them dead. You know anything about that?"

"How would I? Never heard of them."

"Hunter worked off and on as a deputy when I needed him." Longstreet's glance was sharp and piercing. "He was there to help me take Tennant out the day we hanged him. And you're sure you've never been to Bar Cross Bar?"

"Just what are you driving at, Longstreet?"

"I saw a funny thing out there. Four stakes driven into the earth with pieces of rawhide still tied to each one. Like a man had been staked out Indian-fashion. Was that man you, Driscoll?"

"Why would it be me?"

"I knew Otis Hunter," Longstreet said, "I knew him good. He was a greedy buzzard but a tough man, which is why I used him as deputy. I know he's searched for that money. He probably figured, like so many others, that Tennant told you where it was hid. So somehow he and his partner jumped you and staked you out to make you tell. Is that how it was, Driscoll?"

Driscoll shrugged. "If you know so much, why bother to ask me?"

"Somebody shot those two boys," Longstreet said darkly. "I aim to find out who did it."

"Maybe they shot each other."

"Sure. And after they were both dead they dragged each other into a shed."

Driscoll said nothing. He stood there, tense and wary under Longstreet's keen and baleful look. "All I need is one witness, boy," Longstreet went on, "just one witness, one tiny bit of proof and I'll hang you like I hanged Tennant. So if you're smart you'll get your things from Quarter Circle Six and then ride. North, south, east or west, ride fast and far. I'm being good to you, boy, warning you like this. You better heed me."

Longstreet turned and started up the slope with long strides, spurs jangling harshly. He disappeared into the trees and a moment later there came the sound of a running horse. Driscoll listened to the hoofbeats fade and die while his ears still echoed Longstreet's words: Just one witness . . .

He thought of Lee Fairchild then. The man was not to be trusted. Though he had been involved he was clever enough to twist things so that the full blame would fall on Driscoll.

After a while he retrieved his running iron, made sure the branding fire was out, and climbed aboard the black.

Montana watched him riding in. The old man sat on the bench in front of the bunkshack. Montana was grinning.

Driscoll rode past the house and headed for the corrals. He had just dismounted when he heard the door of the house open. He glanced that way and saw Hazel Tennant step outside.

"Will you come over here, Driscoll?" she called. Her tone was flat, commanding. "You needn't bother to unsaddle."

Something chill and prescient passed through Driscoll. Then he had an inkling of what this was all about and he felt anger flare and begin to rise in him.

He walked with slow steps toward the woman. She stood there impatiently, drumming a toe against the ground. Her face looked pale and tired.

"I'm sorry, Driscoll. You'll have to leave."

She stared past him into the distance. He saw the boy watching him warily through a crack in the back door.

He asked quietly, "Isn't my work satisfactory?"

Her head dropped so that he could not see her expression. She made a small, faint sound that could have been exasperation or sorrow.

"I run Quarter Circle Six. It's sufficient to tell you that I don't want you here any more."

He stared at her and felt the beginning of a great, strange tenderness. His mind searched furiously for words to comfort her, but his mind found nothing. Almost without knowing that he was doing so, he reached out a hand. She sensed the movement and dropped back a step and stood watching him with wide, startled eyes, tense and ready to flee.

"I know why you're talking to me like this," Driscoll said. "You needn't fret for me. I told you that once already. I know what I'm up against. I still want to stay."

"No," she whispered. "No. Please, Driscoll."

"I don't scare easy," he said, and found that his voice had turned hard. "I know what happened to your other riders. You needn't blame yourself for anything that happens to me."

"No, Driscoll. You've got to go."

"I won't."

Her face turned stern. "Quarter Circle Six is mine. I order you to leave."

"I still won't go."

"Don't make me say it, Driscoll."

"Say what?"

She drew in her breath in a long, moaning sound and looked past him again. He saw the haunting shadows gather in her eyes, then the tears gathered.

"Every time I see you I remember him. Even before you came I always remembered him. There hasn't been a day since he died that I haven't remembered. I could see him in every room, in every building, in the corrals, riding in at sundown. So I came to Quarter Circle Six.

"Still I was beginning to forget a little. It didn't hurt so much when I remembered. Then you came and now I remember stronger than ever. You bring too much hurt to me. Every time I see you I also see him. Now do you know how it is, Driscoll? Now will you go?"

He put his few belongings in his warsack and then rolled his blankets. Montana entered the bunkshack and stood watching him.

Driscoll picked up his bedroll under one arm and his warsack in the other hand.

"I told you," Montana said, gloating. "I told you you wouldn't last."

"Don't ride me, Montana."

"There are ways of taking care of smart young fellers like you. I told you there was, didn't I? *He-he-he.*"

Driscoll stopped so abruptly his spurs shrilled. "Were you the one, Montana? Were you the one who told Longstreet I was working here?"

The old man shrank back until he touched the wall. His eyes widened. "How could I? How could I tell Longstreet that?"

"You were in Santa Loma, weren't you?"

"But that was before you started working here. I didn't know nothing about that until I came back from town. And I ain't set foot off Quarter Circle Six since."

"You could've told Longstreet I'd been here the day before and so he was laying for me. Is that what you told him?"

The old man began to slide along the wall, moving toward his bunk. Driscoll moved with him and Montana halted.

"You're imagining things, Driscoll. You eat loco weed? I'm just a poor old man, sick with the miseries. I ain't ever said a word against any man in all my life."

"You lie, Montana."

The old man cringed and coughed. "I feel poorly. That's why you pick on me. You heard what Miz Tennant told you. Get off of Quarter Circle Six."

"You'll tell me everything I want to know, Montana."

The old man edged a little more along the wall. "I don't know nothing. I can't tell you nothing."

"You're Longstreet's man, aren't you?"

"Wha-at?"

"You heard me. You're Longstreet's spy."

The old man made a hasty sign on his breast.

"Cross my heart, I ain't. Honest. I swear it, Driscoll."

"Longstreet keeps you here so you can report on everything Mrs. Tennant does. He keeps you here so you can tell him who comes and goes. Isn't that right?"

"You've got me all wrong, Driscoll. It ain't nothing at all like that." Montana coughed and wheezed. "I'm sick. Miz Tennant feels sorry for me. She's a good, holy woman, Driscoll. She's the finest woman I ever did see. She knows what it's like for poor Montana, and she gives me a place to sleep and feeds me. You think I'd turn on a woman like that?"

"You bet I do. You're nothing but a sniveling, lying old drunk. You never did an honest day's work in your life. You lie easier than you tell the truth, but I'm making you tell me everything that Longstreet's done to Mrs. Tennant."

"Please, Driscoll," Montana pleaded, holding up supplicating hands. "You wouldn't hit a poor old man, would you?"

He moved so suddenly that he caught Driscoll by surprise. Before Driscoll could drop his war-sack and bedroll Montana was past him, grunting and sobbing with fright and effort. He reached his bunk and grabbed the Henry rifle off the wall and came around, leveling the weapon.

Driscoll leaped ahead and swept out an arm, knocking the rifle aside before Montana could fire. Fury raged in Driscoll. He grabbed the rifle with both hands and twisted violently. Montana cried out sharply as the Henry was torn from him.

Driscoll grabbed the rifle by the barrel and with both hands brought the stock down on the floor. The stock splintered and another smash broke it off. Driscoll tossed the useless rifle into a corner and moved in to strike Montana. Then shame and remorse brought sanity back to Driscoll. His hand fell without touching Montana. Driscoll picked up his warsack and bedroll again.

"Please, Driscoll," Montana sobbed, raising his head again. "You know where that money is. Just a few dollars. To take me back to Montana, to go to the Bitter Roots and die. Please, Driscoll."

Driscoll started for the door. Behind him he heard Montana start after him. Driscoll walked faster.

"I'll do anything you want me to, Driscoll, if you'll take me in with you. I know lots of things. I can help you, Driscoll, if you'll let me and give me just a little of that money."

Driscoll neither paused nor slowed. The black, still saddled, saw him coming and whinnied.

Driscoll tied his bedroll to the cantle and hung his warsack from the horn. He mounted and turned the black.

Driscoll threw a look at the house as he rode by. The door was closed, the curtains drawn. He lifted the black into a lope and headed westward, toward the Sombras.

CHAPTER 8

Where the Sombras began he pitched his camp in a grove of junipers. At last he was free to ride without forever watching his backtrail. At last he was free to sleep without fear of ambush. So he surrendered himself completely to weariness and slept the profound slumber of exhaustion.

He slept so heavily that he did not hear the black snort and whinny softly in alarm. He was not aware of the man creeping stealthily in through the trees, guided by the beacon of the dying fire.

The man came in carefully. He held his breath as he neared Driscoll's blankets and very quietly lifted the pistol from its holster and then took the rifle from where it lay beside Driscoll. Then the man sighed loudly, not caring how much noise he made. He grinned as he looked at Driscoll.

The man squatted on his heels not far from Driscoll and reached out with Driscoll's rifle and poked him with the barrel. Driscoll mumbled something in his sleep but did not waken. The man poked harder, roughly.

Driscoll awoke abruptly, sitting up and reaching for his weapons. Only when his groping fingers found the empty holster did Driscoll realize what had happened. His eyes cleared and he saw the man squatting there, smiling at him.

"Gently, Davey, lad, gently," Lee Fairchild said.

Driscoll threw the blankets from his legs and started to rise. Fairchild cocked the pistol he had taken from Driscoll and pointed it at him.

"Gently, lad. No need to make any sudden movements." The smile was gone. The bearded face was set hard and solemn. "You might put some wood on the fire, but slowly, lad, very slowly. Remember how my trigger finger has always itched, Davey, lad?"

Driscoll built up the fire and stared at Fairchild.

"Where you headed for, Davey, lad?"

Bitterness came out in Driscoll's voice. "To the other side of the Sombras."

"For sure, this time?"

Driscoll peered at the man. "What you mean?"

"You started to leave two-three nights ago, didn't you? But you turned back."

Sudden revelation came to Driscoll. "It was you that night, trying to sneak in on me."

Fairchild chuckled. "You damn near tagged me a couple of times with all that wild shooting. But I kept an eye on you. I saw you go back to Quarter Circle Six." Eagerness and cupidity made Fairchild's voice sharp and tight. "You've finally got it, haven't you, Davey, lad?"

A feeling of revulsion swept over Driscoll. Everywhere he turned, everywhere he went he encountered this clutching, deadly avarice. "I've had enough of this, Lee," he said. "I've finally realized it was a mistake to come back here."

The pistol held steady in Fairchild's hand. "Are you trying to tell me you haven't got it, Davey, lad?"

"Search me. Search my things."

Fairchild was silent while he ran something over in his mind. "All right. You haven't got it. But you know where it is."

"You make me sick, Lee," Driscoll said wearily. "I don't know a damn thing about that money."

"I might make you sick," Fairchild said, "but you'll be a hell of a lot sicker if you don't tell me."

"What makes you think I know?" Driscoll asked steadily.

"You wouldn't be leaving if you didn't. You hung around long enough to find out where it is. I know you haven't got it with you. But you're on your way to pick it up. Once you have it you'll cross the Sombras. You were on your way the other night when I scared you off. You knew someone was watching you so you went back. Now you're trying it again. But from now on, Davey, lad, you and me, we stick together."

Driscoll sighed. "Stick with me if you want to but it won't do you any good."

"I never waste my time. You know that, Davey, lad. I waited patiently for three years. Now my patience is gone. You'll tell me, Davey, if I have to wrap you in a wet hide and let it dry and squeeze the living breath out of you. It's either split with me or be squeezed to death in a drying hide."

A chill laced the back of Driscoll's neck. "Have it your way, then," he said quietly and edged a hand toward the fire. "But there's nothing I can tell you."

Fairchild opened his mouth to speak when the black whinnied. A moment later a horse answered from within the junipers. Fairchild tensed, straining to hear. He held his breath and when it gusted out Driscoll heard it. He smiled.

Fairchild's answering grin was savage. "It's just my horse, Davey, lad. My sorrel. I've got him hitched out there."

The black began to pace restlessly. Driscoll asked softly, "Can you tell your sorrel's neigh?"

Fairchild made a jeering sound. "You don't trick me that easy, Davey." But he was still listening for something stirring in the junipers.

"You don't think there could be anyone else out there? Don't think you're the only one after that money. If you've been keeping a watch on me, then you saw me and Longstreet today. Did you miss that, Lee?"

"Longstreet?" The word was a hoarse whisper. For a moment Fairchild canted his head toward the junipers. Then he laughed softly. "Longstreet's

111

in Santa Loma. I made sure there was no one on my backtrail."

As if in mocking refutation the whinny came anew from within the trees and the black answered, nickering loudly. Fairchild could not help a quick glance, searching the darkness for what he could not see. Driscoll had bargained for no more chance than this.

He had edged his hand back until it touched a piece of wood sticking out of the fire. He grabbed the end now and flung the flaming brand at Fairchild. A cry of alarm tore out of Fairchild as he saw the burning stick coming at his face.

The pistol blasted, but the slug screamed up at the stars. Fairchild threw an arm up to shield his face. The brand deflected off his elbow then fell amid a shower of sparks.

In the same flow of movement, Driscoll lunged for Fairchild. He reached Fairchild as the man was leveling the pistol for another shot. Driscoll's arm knocked the gun aside and the force of Driscoll's rush carried them back sprawling in a tangle of thrashing arms and legs.

Fairchild swung at Driscoll's head with the barrel of the pistol. Driscoll swerved but took the blow on the base of his neck. Dull pain throbbed there as he reached for Fairchild's right wrist, catching it in both hands and twisting. The weapon fell.

Fairchild struck with his spurs, raking one down

Driscoll's thigh. The pain made Driscoll slacken his hold on Fairchild's wrist. The man tore his arm free and belted Driscoll in the face with both fists. The blows drove Driscoll off and in that moment Fairchild was on him with a swarming lunge.

Fairchild tried to stab his fingers into Driscoll's eyes, but Driscoll reached up and grabbed two fistfuls of Fairchild's long hair and yanked with all his might. Fairchild yelped and started to roll away.

Driscoll rolled with the man, still hanging on to Fairchild's hair. The two cursing men rocked to their feet. Fairchild pelted Driscoll's middle with hard blows that ripped pained grunts out of him but Driscoll hung on to Fairchild's hair. Driscoll pivoted and propelled Fairchild toward the fire. Sticking out his leg, Driscoll tripped Fairchild and the man went sprawling on his stomach into the red embers.

He shrieked again, in pain and fright, and went rolling along the ground, slapping at the burning patches on his clothes. Driscoll scooped up the fallen pistol and leveled it at Fairchild who had finally come to a stop and lay moaning on the ground, wisps of smoke rising from the burnt spots on his clothing.

Driscoll stepped ahead swiftly and pulled Fairchild's pistol from its holster. Then Driscoll stepped back.

"All right, Lee," Driscoll said. "Get up."

The man rose. His eyes never left Driscoll's face. "I'll get you, Dave. I promise you that. I'll get you if it's the last thing I do."

"If I put a bullet in your brain you'll do no getting at all."

Fairchild spat at Driscoll's feet, then started away toward his horse. Driscoll moved after him, pistol still leveled.

"I aim to take your saddle gun," Driscoll said. "I just don't trust you."

They moved into the junipers. When they came to Fairchild's horse the man stood aside while Driscoll pulled the rifle from the saddle-boot. Then Fairchild mounted and without a word rode away.

Morning found Driscoll riding south, following the foot of the Sombras. In a night of thinking he had come to realize that he could never cross the Sombras and leave this range until the matter of the stolen money was settled.

A woman's grief and tears rode with him. He heard her sad voice in the soft crying of the wind. A small boy's loneliness and loss kept him melancholy company. These two would know no relief until that money was found. Only then would the terror flee, the persecution cease.

He skirted Santa Loma, taking care that no one saw him, and rode on south through the red hills. The land leveled off. He came upon the S. P.

tracks and followed the gleaming rails into Fort Britt.

He rode slowly down the main drag with the afternoon sun on him. The black was weary; dust and sweat caked the horse's flanks. Driscoll eyed the street on either side of him, taking in the buildings, the dwellings and stores and saloons.

When he passed the bank he could not help but turn in the saddle for a good look. The door was padlocked, the windows were boarded, the abode brick structure slumbered the unused, cobwebbed, musty sleep of abandonment.

At the livery he reined in the black and then dismounted and led the horse through the wide door. From the hostler Driscoll ordered a rubdown and a feeding of grain for the black and then unsaddled the horse himself and placed it in a stall. He could feel the old man's glance on him, peering, searching, but somehow these glances did not bother Driscoll so much any more.

He went to the wide door and stood there a while, staring down the main drag of Fort Britt and trying to determine just how he would go about the thing. At last he decided that the old barnman was as good a person to start on as anybody.

"Didn't you have a bank robbery in this town about three-four years back?" Driscoll asked.

The old man's eyes sharpened. He nodded.

"I noticed the bank boarded up," Driscoll said.

"That's what made me remember. As I recollect, there was quite a bit of money taken in that robbery."

"Put the bank out of business," the old man said.

"They ever find it?"

The eyes watched Driscoll with a chill consideration. The old man shrugged. "Some say they have and others say they haven't. Take your pick."

"Didn't they hang a man for it?" Driscoll asked, and had to wince inside at the memory.

"Yup. Jim Tennant. Served him right. There's a few who were sorry for him but not me. He got what he had coming."

Driscoll sensed the animosity, the deep hatred, and something soured in him. "Well, do a good job on that black."

Driscoll walked to the end of town, wondering what he expected to find here. He had already seen all there was to see, the bank moldering and standing as a monument to bitterness and greed and anguish. There was nothing else in Fort Britt.

He wandered on until he came to the small hill which held the cemetery. For a while he walked among the graves, staring down at the markers. Only one name registered on his brain. John Sloane. He recalled that as the name of the banker whom Tennant had pistol whipped when they wouldn't believe he was serious about the holdup.

"Are you Mr. Driscoll?"

Driscoll whirled swiftly, reaching instinctively

for his pistol, and then he saw that it was only a boy of twelve or so and felt foolish. It was not surprising that he had been recognized. He remembered that there had been quite a few people in the courtroom the day of his sentencing. Some of those people had undoubtedly been from Fort Britt. Now the news of his presence here was all over town.

"That's right, son," he said quietly.

The boy looked pale and frightened. "I come on an errand. Someone wants to see you. I'm supposed to show you the way."

"Who is it, son?" Driscoll asked quietly.

"Old Mrs. Sloane."

He felt uncomfortable and ill at ease and it was not because the chair in which he was sitting was hard and unpadded. The cup and saucer in his hand were beautiful, fragile things, and he was in constant fear of dropping them or having them crumble in his grip. He was used to tin cups and plates that you could straighten out if they ever bent or dented.

"John and I were very proud of our many beautiful things." Her smile was tender and nostalgic with remembrance. "You see, we had no children. So we collected beautiful things to brighten up our home . . . After—after our misfortune John sold our home and all our beautiful things to fulfill his obligations incurred by the failure of the bank. He sold them, all but these pieces of Dresden china. I wanted him to sell these, too, because I knew how much he wanted to make up the losses to the depositors. But he would not part with these and made me promise never to part with them. They were his wedding present to me."

She sat there across from him, very quiet, very small, watching him with bright, smiling eyes. There was no more than a touch of sadness in her voice. Her life had been full though some precious things had been denied her but she did not rue her misfortunes. She dwelt on the pleasant memories most of all and did her waiting in this small, shabby house.

"More coffee, Mr. Driscoll?"

"No. No, thanks."

She took the cup and saucer and he noticed her hands were small and worn red from many launderings. He imagined those hands in happier days when they must have been very soft and pale and beautiful. She returned and sat and folded her hands in her lap and peered brightly at him.

"I imagine you are wondering why I asked you here."

He nodded.

"I have heard many stories about you, especially during the past few days. When I learned you were in Fort Britt—that information, incidentally, is all over town—I invited you here because I wanted to look at you. I am glad I did. You are not at all like I was led to believe you were. I am quite sure of that."

Embarrassment made him lower his eyes. He sat mute and disconcerted.

"Many people have sought that money from the bank," she went on. "Everyone says that is the reason you came back to this range. There are those who say that Mr. Tennant told you where he had hidden that money. That is possible, but I do not believe it."

He lifted his glance and looked at her now. Something strange and wonderful and gentle began to stir in him. Before, he had always been at odds and combat with the world and its people. All at once he could no longer understand or see a reason for such perverseness.

"How can you be so sure?" he asked quietly. "You never saw me before today. You know what I was."

Her smile was gentle and compassionate. "It takes a lonely person to understand another lonely one, Mr. Driscoll."

There had never been anyone who had ever looked into him in such a way and seen the truth hidden there in the dark, distant corners of himself. But she had.

"I really believe that money means nothing to you," she went on. "You did not come back here because of that. You came back to help someone. That is why I admire you, Mr. Driscoll."

He had never been at such a loss for something to say. She could read him as if every thought, every emotion were written in bold letters on his features.

"I would like to help Mrs. Tennant, too, although I do not know what I could do," she continued when he had nothing to say. "John went to see her once. You see, John tried everything to recover that money to make good his obligations. He told me later that he hardly more than greeted her. The wound was still raw. He could see that in her eyes. So he did not ask her any of the things he wanted to ask. That is why I have never approached her. There would be too many memories, for both of us."

"I'd like to find that money," he said slowly. "I'd like to find it because then it would end everything that's hanging over her."

"But what if she is the one who knows the secret? What if she wants to keep that money for herself?"

"I don't think she knows the secret."

"Who knows it then? Mr. Tennant killed a man and hurt many lives when he stole that money. He did it for a reason. He did not do it just to let that money rot somewhere. Do you know why he stole that money, Mr. Driscoll?"

"He told me he did it for his wife and boy."

She nodded. "I have much time to think, Mr. Driscoll. So it has been apparent to me for some time that there is only one person Mr. Tennant would have entrusted his secret to. Have you ever considered the boy, Mr. Driscoll?"

He sat there stunned. Yet when he thought back on it, it was the only logical conclusion. He had been blind, but would others be as blind?

"But the boy is so young. He'd have been only about eight at the time."

"I understand he is a rather strange, solemn boy. People credit that to the tragedy that struck his family. I believe otherwise, Mr. Driscoll. I believe the secret weighs heavily on him."

"You mean Tennant trusted his son over his wife?"

She smiled sadly, understandingly. "There could have been several reasons. Perhaps he did not fully trust his wife. Perhaps he feared she would become conscience-stricken and return the money. The boy was young and impressionable. He was undoubtedly very close to his father. The boy was sworn to secrecy and has kept the secret."

He could feel panic rise in him. "Do you think any one else suspects it's the boy?"

For the first time a cloud passed over the patient, gentle features. "I have told no one," she whispered. "I have not known what to do. But I pray every night that no one suspects it's the boy. I would not want him harmed. Too much hurt has already been done because of that money."

"You've told me," Driscoll said.

"Yes," she said, and smiled anew. "I know I have."

CHAPTER 9

He neared his destination with dawn breaking pale and cloudless in the east. The black snorted and coughed tiredly. Driscoll could hear the thumping of the horse's heart as he reined it in and sat in the saddle, watching the buildings of Quarter Circle Six take shape and substance in the dawn.

No light glowed anywhere and he did not expect any at this hour. He rode in slowly, cared for his horse. When he turned from this he found Hazel Tennant emerging from the house.

He watched her approach. Her eyes were still swollen with drowsiness. "I thought you had left for good," she said.

"I changed my mind."

"You know what seeing you does to me, don't you?" Tears gathered in her eyes, but he knew the truth behind them now. They were not for the memories but for something else.

"You said that the other day because you knew it was the only thing that would make me leave Quarter Circle Six." He took a deep breath. "It isn't like that at all. As for memories, there are lots of things and people to make you remember even more than I do. I won't go away any more, Hazel."

He saw her start slightly. She colored a little and looked at the ground.

"The sheriff—" she began, then could not continue.

"Let me worry about Longstreet."

"I couldn't ask you, or anyone, to risk his life for me." Her glance rose and locked with his. "And you would be risking it. You know that, don't you?"

He felt a breath of anger. "Longstreet's had his way long enough. He's terrorized you and the boy long enough. He doesn't want that money to return it. He wants it for himself."

She peered at him. "Why do you say that? No one has ever questioned his honesty. He's brutal but he's honest."

"I know for a fact," Driscoll said, remembering a night and the whispering. "If I wasn't sure of it, I wouldn't have come back."

"All right, Driscoll," she said in a barely audible voice. "But if anything happens to you I'll blame myself."

He saw the gathering of the tears again but she turned and was going quickly toward the house. A sound drifted back, a stifled sob, an echo of pain . . .

He told Montana, "You keep your distance. Don't you say one word to me. You rile me once more, Montana, and Longstreet or no, you'll have to find yourself another place to bunk. I promise you that."

The old man spread his hands pleadingly and his mouth worked but no sounds emanated. Fear shone bright in his eyes.

That morning Driscoll greased the windmill. He climbed down from the tower to find the boy standing some distance away, watching him. The boy had his father's pistol and gunbelt. The belt was much too large for the boy's waist and so he had looped the belt over his shoulder, bandolier style.

Driscoll smiled at the boy. "Come over here, Billy. Let's sit down and have a talk."

The boy did not stir or speak. Driscoll felt sadness come and a touch of loneliness. The somber eyes watched him unblinkingly. He walked toward the boy, half-expecting him to run, but the boy stood his ground. Now Driscoll could glimpse the wariness in the boy's glance, the suspicion and distrust. Sarah Sloane was right about the boy knowing.

Driscoll dropped to one knee. "That's a nice pistol you've got there, Billy."

The boy looked down at the sixshooter in his hands with pride. "My Pa give it to me. He said for me to keep it always to remember him by." The boy's glance lifted. "And I will," he said fiercely, eyes suddenly burning. "I'll never forget him."

"Could I see that pistol, Billy?"

The boy recoiled as though a poisonous snake had been thrust at him. He clutched the pistol to his chest. "It's mine. No one's taking it from me."

"I'm not trying to take it from you. I just want to look at it. I'll let you look at mine as soon as I unload it."

"I won't. It's mine. You might not give it back to me. You can keep your dirty old pistol. I don't want to look at it. My Pa give this pistol to me and no one's taking it from me."

"All right, Billy," Driscoll said, feeling the sadness again. "But let's be friends. Can't we be that?"

"I got no friends," the boy said fiercely. "I don't want none, either."

He turned and trotted toward the house, the holster bobbing at his side.

He saw Montana come into the bunkshack and give him a look and a grin. He wondered instantly because for the first time that day there was no fear in the old man's eyes, no groveling in his manner. Then Driscoll heard the sounds of a horse coming into the yard.

Something tightened in him as he went to the door. Longstreet threw a long shadow in the setting sun as he walked toward the bunkshack, spurs proclaiming his approach loudly. All at once

125

Driscoll regretted having removed his shell belt. It was hanging with his holstered pistol on a peg above his bunk. When he turned that way he saw that Montana had the pistol. The old man pointed it at Driscoll and grinned.

"He-he-he," Montana said.

Something sank in Driscoll. He turned around and saw that Longstreet was smiling, too, the puma smile.

"You wouldn't take my advice, would you, Driscoll?"

"What is this?" Driscoll growled, watching as Longstreet opened the handcuffs.

"Put out your hands, boy."

"What for?"

"I'm putting these irons on you."

"I want to know what for."

"Blast him, Montana, if he don't obey me pronto."

"He-he-he," Montana said. The pistol clicked as he cocked it.

Driscoll thrust out his hands. The cuffs bit into the flesh of his wrists as Longstreet snapped them shut. Driscoll winced and Longstreet grinned.

"All right," Driscoll said quietly. "Now you've got the irons on me. Tell me what you're taking me in for. I have a right to know that."

"Vagrancy, boy."

"How can you charge me with that when I'm working?"

Longstreet's brows arched in a great show of astonishment. "Working? Where?"

"Here. Where the hell else?"

"Didn't Miz Tennant fire you?"

"I'm still here. Isn't that enough?"

"How about it, Montana?"

"She fired him, all right," the old man said. "Two days ago."

"But she hired me back."

"Did she, boy?"

They heard her coming then, soft, quick steps whispering against the packed earth of the yard. Driscoll caught her anxious glance.

The sheriff drew his Stetson from his head. All at once his manner became obsequious. "Howdy, Miz Hazel," Longstreet said, voice quiet and humble. "This gent won't be bothering you any more."

Her lips moved stiffly. "What has he done?"

Longstreet shrugged. "Didn't you order him to leave Quarter Circle Six the other day?"

The woman nodded. Fear-flecked eyes darted to Driscoll, then away. She seemed gripped both by terror and shame.

"Well, I'm just going to lock him up so he won't come bothering you any more."

"Couldn't you let him go if he promised to leave the county and never return?" the woman asked.

"Well, I don't rightly know," Longstreet said, scratching the side of his neck. "I've already tried

127

reasoning with him. I warned him two-three times to move on but he just won't listen, Miz Hazel. His kind got to learn the hard way."

"Please," she said.

"Now, Miz Hazel, don't you go pleading with me. I got a job to do. I do my duty all the time. I don't grant favors to anybody."

The woman turned to Driscoll. "Promise him you won't come back here any more. Promise you'll leave the county. Won't you do that, Driscoll?"

"That won't do any good. Just tell him you've hired me. He can't jail me for vagrancy then. Tell the judge that when he brings me up for a hearing. Will you do that, Mrs. Tennant?"

Longstreet's face turned dark. The fawning fled from him. "You pay him any money in wages yet, Miz Hazel?"

"No."

"You got any money to pay him?"

She shook her head.

"He couldn't work for you then, could he? No man works for nothing. He's told you something, hasn't he? Something to scare you into letting him stay here. Isn't that right, Montana?"

"You bet," the old man said. "I'll get right up in court and swear to that. Right on the Bible, I will. He's got her really scared of him, Sheriff."

Longstreet spread his hands. "There you are, Miz Hazel. I'm doing you a favor. He's a thief and an ex-convict. So don't defend him. With his record there's no telling what he might do. You wouldn't want to take a chance on any harm coming to your boy, would you?"

The woman's face paled still more, "No," she whispered. "I wouldn't want that."

"All right," Longstreet said. "I'm glad you see how it is. You'll never regret this, Miz Hazel."

She threw a look at Driscoll. He thought there was a plea in it, an asking for forgiveness, but he did not care. She turned and walked away without a word of farewell. He watched her go up the steps and shut the door without once looking back.

"All right, boy," Longstreet said. "Let's get moving."

The combination jail and courthouse in Santa Loma loomed dark and forbidding, dungeon-like against the gloom and the stars. Longstreet dismounted and motioned for Driscoll to do the same. On the ground Driscoll stretched stiffly. The cuffs bit into his wrists. His hands were numb.

Longstreet told Driscoll to move with a jerk of the head. Longstreet followed, carrying Driscoll's shell belt and pistol and saddle gun. The deputy opened the door and Driscoll passed inside with Longstreet on his heels.

"You can go now, Pete," Longstreet told the deputy. "Put the horses up at the livery. Tell the barnman the black will be there a long, long time."

The deputy threw a strange, peering look at Driscoll, then was gone without a word. Longstreet closed the door behind him and then put the rifle in a rack on the wall and placed the pistol in a drawer of his desk. Then he picked up a set of leg irons and held them with the shackles in one hand and the chain swinging free.

"You know the way, Driscoll." There was a sharp, avid look in the pale yellow eyes.

"You gonna put leg irons on me, too?" Driscoll growled, no longer trying to contain his anger. "What the hell's the big idea? All you're holding me on is a vagrancy charge."

There was a flat, hard expression on Longstreet's face. "You gonna move, boy, or you need a push?"

Driscoll turned and started for the cell-block door. The squealing of the chain warned him but he had no more time than to tense. The chain struck him high on his back and sent him slamming up against the door.

He rolled and started to fall as another blow struck him and then he was on the floor with his arms and hands shielding his face and Longstreet towering and raging above him.

"I told you and I told you," Longstreet was snarling, "don't ever make me get you in my jail again, I told you. But no, you wouldn't listen. You'll listen after this."

The chain squealed anew and came crashing down but Driscoll threw himself forward. He rolled up hard against Longstreet, upsetting the sheriff's balance enough so that the man fell back two reeling steps. As Driscoll started to rise, however, Longstreet recovered swiftly and came in with a rush, chain clanking.

There was no avoiding this blow, though Driscoll ducked. By throwing up his hands he warded the chain off his face but a link rapped him high on the head and sent him reeling and falling again, and a darkness darted at him. But he fended off the black and sought the shelter of the desk, going around it on all fours with Longstreet in pursuit.

"You think you're going to get that money?" Longstreet was raving. "You think you can get her to tell by hanging around Quarter Circle Six? I've waited too long, boy, too long to let any one take that away from me. I gave you more than enough fair warning. Now you're paying, boy, you're paying."

He sensed Longstreet stooping over him to get a better blow at him and Driscoll lashed out suddenly with his boots, catching Longstreet in the shins, and as the man stiffened and cried out, Driscoll raked him across the thighs with his spurs. Another cry of pain tore out of Longstreet and drove him back. Driscoll rose weaving and made for the door.

He had his fingers on the knob, he was turning it, the breath sobbing and laboring in his aching throat, when Longstreet got him again. This blow brought the darkness back with a great, plunging rush and he felt himself hurtling, cascading into an abyss.

He did not know when the blows stopped. He had expected them to continue without mercy until he made the one last great descent into oblivion, but he felt the blackness lift anew and began to know pain more and more. In the jungle of his consciousness there seemed to be many sounds, of scuffling, and voices, and wrath, and something being flung with a crash.

Hands reached for him and he cried out angrily in the blindness of his hurt and lashed them away. But the voice kept calling him, saying his name, and finally some of the agony washed out of his eyes and he could see a crazy, spinning, red-tinted world and a featureless face over him.

"Dave. It's me, Dave. Don't you hear me, Dave?"

The face above him cleared and he could see without a doubt who it was.

"Noel," he whispered, and felt blood trickling down his cheeks. "Noel."

Reese had a bandanna in his hand and gently dabbed at the blood on Driscoll's face, but the black anger came now to Driscoll and he struck Reese's hand away and sought to rise.

"Where is he?" he growled. "Get these irons off me and then show me where he is."

"Here are the keys, Noel," a strange voice said.

As Reese bent to unlock the handcuffs, Driscoll looked over Reese's shoulder and saw Fred Duchaine holding a gun on Longstreet.

"You know this is breaking a man out of jail," Longstreet said to Duchaine.

Duchaine stood squat and short, red with anger. "This man has no cause to be in jail."

"I can hold him overnight, can't I?" Longstreet growled, the glitter in his pale yellow eyes betraying the fury raging in him. "I was going to bring him up before the judge in the morning, charge him with vagrancy."

"How can you charge him with that when he's working?"

Longstreet's eyes narrowed. "Working where?"

Duchaine answered softly, "For Half Moon. For me."

Driscoll's wrists were free. He sought to stand, rose halfway, and would have toppled if Reese had not caught him. "Easy, Dave," Reese whispered, holding Driscoll back from Longstreet. "You're in no shape to tackle him now. Take it easy now."

Longstreet's eyes stayed fixed on Duchaine. His voice was soft.

"Then how come I found him at Quarter Circle Six?"

"I hired him this morning. He'd left some things there and went to get them."

"You're a liar, Duchaine," Longstreet said without a change in tone.

"You're a liar, too," Duchaine said in the same voice, "and should we talk about that a while?"

"So you bought into this game," Longstreet said to Duchaine, "you and your rider. Well, that's all right with me. I'm happier this way. Now I know for sure where you stand."

"You always did know where I stood," Duchaine said.

"That's right. But you always kept your nose out of my business. Now you've dirtied it, and I promise you it'll get dirtied a lot more before I get through with you."

Duchaine made a sign at the door to Reese. Reese tugged at Driscoll's arm but he would not go. His eyes were rigid on Longstreet.

"Stay out of my way, Longstreet," Duchaine said, "and off my ranch. Stay away from my daughter."

A hint of color touched the crests of Longstreet's cheeks. The growl returned to his voice. "I was never anything but civil with her. I will keep on being that way with her. I will stop talking to her only when she tells me so herself."

"I tolerated you on my place before," Duchaine said. "I won't do so any more." He motioned again at the door. "Get him out of here, Noel."

"No." The word burst hoarsely out of Driscoll. He made a lunge at Longstreet and a great rush of blackness all but sent him sprawling. "No." He almost wept the word. Reese caught him and supported him and as Driscoll's vision cleared again he found Longstreet grinning that puma grin at him.

"Let's go, son," Duchaine said gently. "You'll have your day another time. I've got your guns. You'll have them back. Let's go now, son."

Outside, the night air revived Driscoll. He drew it in with great, gulping, rasping breaths. And now with the wrath no longer tormenting him the pain began to glow . . .

Reese rode close beside him, supporting him every time he sagged or reeled in the saddle. Duchaine rode behind, casting frequent looks over his shoulder, but no one came barreling after them out of Santa Loma.

When they passed the turn-off to Quarter Circle Six, Driscoll remembered. He reined the black that way and Reese had to jump his bay ahead and grab the black's bridle.

"Let him go," Driscoll shouted with fury. "Damn you. Let my horse go." He launched a swing at Reese and missed and would have pitched headlong out of the saddle if Duchaine hadn't come riding up and caught him.

"Easy, son," Duchaine said soothingly. "We're not there yet. We've got a little ways to Half Moon yet."

"I'm not going to Half Moon. Quarter Circle Six. That's where I'm going."

"There's no one there, son."

Panic rose chattering in Driscoll. "What do you mean there's no one there? She's there. The boy's there. They need me. That beast in town he ain't going to harm them, not if I can help it."

"She's not there, son."

"That's right," Reese said. "She's at Half Moon. She's the one who told us," Duchaine said gently. "She rode over to Half Moon and told us Longstreet had taken you away and so me and Noel took off hell-for-leather for town."

"But the boy," Driscoll said, starting to fight them again. "That means the boy is there alone."

"She had the boy with her. He's safe at Half Moon, too. Come along, son. You're with friends now."

Driscoll quieted then. He got a hold on the saddle horn and they started on their way.

CHAPTER 10

When Driscoll first saw the lights of Half Moon he thought they were just flashes of pain before his eyes. But the lights grew and then the buildings took dim form in the darkness and a dog set up a barking and he knew this was no tormented hallucination.

They rode into the yard with the dog growling louder and fiercer. Duchaine said something sharply. The dog growled twice and then subsided. The door of the house opened and Driscoll saw the woman standing there, limned against the lamplight.

Driscoll's heart leaped, then missed a beat when he saw that this woman wore a dress and he recalled that he had never seen Hazel Tennant in anything but men's clothing. The lamplight drew fire from the woman's hair and then she was in the shadows, running toward them.

He stepped down from the saddle with Reese's help and groaned aloud at the hurt the movements inflicted on him.

"Where is she?" He knew he spoke thickly and with difficulty but he was too angry to care. "You said she'd be here. Damn you. Where is she?"

Duchaine tried to soothe him.

"Damn you, Duchaine. Where is she? Where's the boy?"

The girl answered him. "She left, Driscoll. I begged her to stay but she took the boy and left for Quarter Circle Six."

"No." They were leading him to the house but with a sudden burst of violence that almost blanked him out with agony he broke away from them. "She can't go there. She can't stay there any more." He was surprised at how easily and swiftly he could run. Then the earth reached up and slapped him in the face and immediately their hands had him again.

"Easy, son," Duchaine said. "We'll look after her. I'll send Noel to guard her tonight. You do that, Noel, as soon as we get him in the house. Will you come now, Driscoll?"

They steered him toward the house and he went without resisting. "Why didn't she stay here?" he said aloud. "Why did she go back? Why won't she accept the help that's offered her?"

"She's a proud woman, Driscoll," Duchaine said gently. "A proud woman and a hurt one. But we'll look after her. You can depend on that."

At the door Reese left them. Driscoll stopped and Duchaine and the girl stopped with him and waited until the creak of saddle leather came as Reese mounted, and then the quick, sharp running of a horse going south. When the sounds had all but died, Driscoll heeded the girl's gentle pressure on his arm and stepped inside.

When dawn came and the room turned gray, he felt a great tiredness and his eyes grew heavy-lidded and he could feel himself draw apart from the world and this time his surrender to sleep was utter and complete. Once he thought he heard someone enter the room and he could sense the someone standing there, watching him, but he told himself it was just a dream. So he did not even try to open his eyes but slept on in the quiet, peaceful gloom.

When he finally awoke he found himself lying on his back and for a while he lay there, staring up at the ceiling. The room was dim. When he finally dared, he turned his head and saw that the shades were drawn. Then something permeated his nostrils, a sweet, gentle essence, and he quickly turned his head and saw her sitting there, watching him. Her slim hands were folded in her lap and the smile seemed to soften all at once with something just for him.

"How do you feel?"

"I'm fine." He forgot himself and started to move and pain lanced him and made him wince. "I'm all right," he said.

"I've got some coffee on the stove," she said, rising. "I'll get you a cup and then fix you breakfast."

When she was gone, he tried a few movements and winced at each flash of pain. I'm all right, he told himself. I'm just stiff and sore. I've got to be all right. His exertions brought a fine film of sweat to his upper lip.

She returned and placed the steaming cup on the chair beside the bed so that he could reach it. She smiled at him again and left. He tried again, inching his way this time, and after ages of pains and aches he was sitting on the edge of the bed. His clothes were on a chair nearby, and he managed to work his way into his Levi's. His shirt was quite a bit easier and he began to hope until he tried to pull on his boots. This time he groaned aloud before he could check himself.

She appeared in the doorway. The look she gave him was neither surprised nor reproving. She watched him calmly and coolly, unsmiling now.

"You still think you're all right?" she said quietly.

"I'll make it," he said, feeling the sweat run all over him. A moment's giddiness seized him as he started to bend over. Then he straightened and the giddiness passed. "I've got to get out of here."

"Why?"

He stared at her. "You know why."

She made her first sound of exasperation, a soft sigh. "Noel's still there. Father said he would look in Quarter Circle Six this morning to make sure everything's all right. I don't know what you're so worried about."

"Where is your father?"

"Somewhere out on the range. He's got things to do now that Noel's at Quarter Circle Six. I imagine he'll be back sometime this afternoon. Will you stop worrying?"

"I don't like people putting themselves out for me," he said, wondering at the thickness in his throat.

"But it's all right for you to put yourself out for others." She gave him a softly severe look. "As long as you're sitting up I'll bring you your breakfast . . ."

That afternoon when he was alone, he tried again. It was much easier this time. The soreness and stiffness were abating. The sense of gloom and helplessness fled from him.

He got his boots on and was walking about the room, feeling himself growing freer and stronger by the minute, when the door opened and the girl entered. She stopped short when she spied him and he was so happy he could rely on himself again that he grinned at her.

"Don't look so surprised," he told her. "Aren't you glad you'll be getting rid of me?"

He thought he detected a flash of something in her eyes, like fear or distress, and this made him wonder.

"You're always welcome at Half Moon," she said. "Don't you know that?"

Embarrassment made him lower his head. He owed Half Moon and the Duchaines a lot, he was thinking. They were the only people to show him consideration and concern since his return to this range. He knew he could never repay them.

"The more I move the better I feel," he said, mumbling the words. "I think I'll get some air."

She took a step aside to let him pass. Even so he all but brushed against her. The nearness, the sweet and clean scent of her, sent a strong and strange emotion through him, and he was glad when he was past her and heading for the door.

The air on his face felt good. The wind tossed his hair and tugged at his sleeves. He took great, gulping breaths and then stepped down into the yard.

The black spotted him and whinnied from the corral and Driscoll turned that way. The black nickered again and pressed against the corral bars, waiting for him. He stroked the black mane and the soft muzzle and the horse nibbled gently at his fingers.

He was lost in this when he heard the steps behind him. He turned slowly, knowing that strange and fierce emotion again, and fearing it because he could not define its true nature. He stared at her, at the lissom slimness of her, the fine features of her face, the red wind-blown glory of her hair. The emotion came again and all at once he could have wept because she appealed to him so much and because she and her father had already done so much for him.

He could see that strange, anxious look in the blue eyes. "You aren't thinking of going, are you, Dave?"

He peered at her. This was the first time she had used his given name. It was as though she read his thoughts for she colored ever so slightly.

"My place is at Quarter Circle Six," he said simply.

Her head dropped. Her fingers twined about each other. "You must think an awful lot of her," she said, low-voiced.

"It isn't anything at all like that." All of a sudden he wanted to be gentle with her. "She just doesn't have anyone to look after her and the boy. They're alone."

Her head lifted and her eyes caught his and held. "Did Jim Tennant ask you to look after them?"

He pondered the question, then dismissed the doubt angrily. He must tell this girl the truth. "No. He never said a word to me." He knew he had to give some explanation. "It's Longstreet. The kind of man he is and how he goes after things he wants. If it wasn't for him I wouldn't get mixed up in this. I don't even think I'd have come back to this range."

"Yes. Longstreet," she said, and gave a small shudder.

He watched her closely, remembering something now from out of the welter of pain and hate and rage. "Has he ever bothered you?"

She seemed to draw away from him. Her eyes looked at him in a strange, distant way. "How do you mean?"

"Has he—I mean, do you know him very well?"

Her glance moved past him. A small, dry smile touched her mouth and for an instant made it bitter.

"He called on me a few times. He—I've had many callers." She colored faintly and the distant look in her eyes wavered. "He and Father have always disliked each other. Father wants me to marry well." Her glance returned to the present and sought his, boldly, defiantly. "But I'll only marry the man I love," she said with a toss of her head. "I won't care whether he's rich or poor, handsome or ugly. The only thing that will matter will be if I love him. I've told Father that."

"What do you think of Longstreet?" Driscoll asked.

She looked at him with a frown, then giggled suddenly. "Do you think I mean *him?*" she said. Then she sobered and gave that shudder again. "He—he scares me. Just looking at him scares me. But I must say he's always been very polite to me. I can't rightly say that he has ever annoyed me. But even so Father ordered me not to encourage him. As if I'd ever do a thing like that."

"I'm glad to hear that," he said, and knew that his lips moved stiffly and that his voice was cold.

She stared at him with that strange look again. "Would—would it have meant something then to you if he *had* been unpleasant to me?" she whispered.

He felt something swell in his throat. There was a plaintive, wistful look on her face and he found himself taking a step toward her. In a searing instant he saw how desolate an exile he was from the warmth and comfort and consolation of a home and family. Want cried in him and hunger and need. She took a hesitant step toward him and then he had her in his arms and everything that was in him poured into his kiss.

Suddenly the old wariness and reluctance and distrust of everything and everybody intervened. Perhaps it was a certain lack of innocence on her part, that deterred him, too.

She seemed to sense the sudden change in him and she drew back, face flaming, eyes restless and embarrassed. He let her go and tried to catch something sweet and reassuring in her eyes but her glance would not hold still.

The horses in the corral whinnied and from out on the range came an answer. Driscoll felt himself go alert and tense. He had not thought to belt on his pistol and he had a frightening recollection of when the same oversight had cost him his freedom. He had turned for the house when the girl spoke.

"That must be Father."

He came to a stop, slightly ashamed of his violent alarm, and watched Fred Duchaine riding in from around the barn. Duchaine's face broke into a wide smile when he spied Driscoll.

"Well," Duchaine cried. "On your feet, I see. That's wonderful news, son."

Duchaine dismounted. He looked queryingly at his daughter and then at Driscoll, both of them standing silent there. He glanced again at the girl, asking with his eyes.

A little color had gone from the girl's lips. Her face was somber. "Driscoll's leaving us, Father."

"No." Duchaine turned on Driscoll. "You're not well yet. Stay here at least one more night. If you're worried about Mrs. Tennant and the boy," Duchaine said, "they're fine. I just came from there. Noel's looking after them. His orders are to stay there until I tell him different."

"It isn't exactly that," Driscoll said, and dropped his eyes. He became aware that the girl was watching him closely. "Thanks for everything that you and Rosalie have done for me. I've got to go. I can't explain why. I've just got to."

"We'll be seeing you again, won't we?" There was a measure of anxiety in Duchaine's tone.

"Oh, I'll be around. I'll be back," Driscoll said,

trying to make his smile easy and genuine, but when he looked at the girl she did not respond. Her face remained solemn, even bitter. "I'll get the rest of my things now and saddle up."

She followed him into the house while Duchaine stayed outside. She got Driscoll's warsack for him and his bedroll while he took his saddle gun and shell belt and pistol from the room in which he'd slept. He came out, carrying the rifle in one hand, his hat in the other.

She stood by the door, watching him. He stopped in front of her. "Rosalie," he said, striving hard for words, "I don't know how to tell you. But I won't forget you and I'll think about you. I promise."

She finally showed him a small, wan smile. "Be careful, Dave."

"I will."

He picked up his things and went outside. Duchaine watched him in silence while he saddled the black and mounted. He nodded to Duchaine and then to the girl who stood in the doorway, and he headed the black south.

CHAPTER 11

From far off he heard the shots and on the instant his heart twisted and turned to ice. No, he cried silently. Not yet, not when I'm so far away. The shots kept popping like distant, innocent fire-crackers in the quiet of the dying day.

He struck spurs to the black and sent the horse at a swift, reckless run over the land. The shots grew louder as he approached, solitary, scattered shots as though the people involved were sniping at each other.

He pulled the black down to a trot and tried to think. The shots were coming at longer intervals now. While their sounds filled him with dread, they also carried a portent of hope. As long as the shooting persisted, it meant that the attackers had not yet achieved their ends.

He left the black in a draw that ran to the north of the buildings of Quarter Circle Six. He got his saddle gun out of its boot, patted the black once on the neck, then went on on foot.

He thought once of Longstreet and felt his lips draw back from his teeth in a savage, anticipatory snarl. I'll pay you, he thought cruelly, I'll pay you back good.

He was near the buildings now and he climbed

the side of the draw most carefully and from behind a thicket surveyed the buildings and the yard ahead. He lay there on his belly with the rifle gripped in both hands, cursing the sweat that kept dripping down over his eyes.

The shooting was coming from the house. He noted that first of all and felt hope leap in him. Then the optimism died as he noticed the man lying outstretched in the yard. The long white hair stirring in the wind told Driscoll that the man was old Montana, fixed in the slack rigidity of death.

The gun roared again from the house. After the echoes had died away, the sinister silence set in again. Driscoll peered until his eyes ached. There had to be someone out there or that carbine would not be fired at such irregular intervals. It had to be someone now showing himself then darting back to safety, drawing the shots and trying to lure someone in the house into revealing himself.

Driscoll wormed his way along the edge of the draw, hugging the ground, keeping a swell in the land between him and the yard, poking his head up occasionally for a look. At last he saw it, just the hat, a black Stetson, showing briefly around a corner of the water trough by the windmill. The instant the hat showed the carbine cracked and the hat pulled back swiftly.

What's the matter with you, Noel? Driscoll thought angrily. He's just poking that hat out on the barrel of his rifle. Any one but a dumbbell can tell you that. What you wasting cartridges for?

The hat appeared again, slowly, shyly. The carbine cracked anew and the hat disappeared.

Noel, Noel, Driscoll raged silently. He's trying to run you out of ammunition. Can't you tell that . . . Then anguish cried in him and sorrow and fear. That was not Reese, then. And if it was not Reese, then the man must be—

Now the black wrath came with its furious, devastating rush. He went along the ground, hugging the land where he had to, moving on all fours elsewhere, running crouched over when he could, making a great circle while the carbine cracked again.

When he had made his circle and could see and recognize the man behind the tank, he knew a vivid disappointment because it was not Longstreet. The man behind the tank was Lee Fairchild.

Driscoll came up on his knees. Fairchild was starting to poke his hat out again. Driscoll cocked the rifle and put it to his shoulder.

"Lee."

Fairchild froze for the barest instant, then came lashing around like a whipping snake, the swiftness and frenzy of his movements raising dust. The hat flew off his rifle barrel and sailed with the wind.

Driscoll shot him in the stomach.

Fairchild groaned while his face twisted into an anguished grimace. He arched back against the tank, one leg flexing out in front of him. But he hung on to his rifle and started now to raise it.

Driscoll shot him in the chest.

Fairchild collapsed then, like a bellows with the air suddenly let out of it. He flopped on his back and lay there, making small, feeble motions with his hands and legs.

Driscoll gave a swift look about, scanning the yard. Only Montana showed, hair rippling in the wind, and a dust devil skipping across the yard. The gun in the house had ceased.

Driscoll moved in cautiously, rifle held ready at his hip. Fairchild's weapon lay beside him. With his toe Driscoll pushed it aside and stood, looking down at Fairchild.

The man was staring straight up with his wide, lifeless eyes. There was no pity in Driscoll, just the black rage. "For Noel, Lee," he snarled. "For anything you might have done to Noel. How do you like dying for what you've done to him?"

Driscoll took the man's weapons and then hurried toward the house, dreading what he might find. Spare her and the boy, he prayed, her and the boy.

He burst through the door and pulled up sharply, glancing wildly about. There were bullet holes in the walls and shattered glass from the window on the floor. A chair was upset and several broken plates beside it, the shards like fragments of a once beautiful dream.

The boy huddled in a far corner, the pistol held in both hands and pointing at Driscoll. The boy's face was pale with fright, his eyes wide and distended, but there was a grim purpose in the shape of his mouth.

The woman was kneeling beside Reese who lay on his back on the floor. She had given a small cry when Driscoll burst into the room. Now she watched him sadly, pityingly.

Driscoll started ahead.

"I'll shoot," the boy cried, voice tight and shrill. "I'll shoot you if you come any closer to my Ma."

The woman turned on the boy. "Billy. Put down that pistol. It's Driscoll. He helped us. He's on our side."

The boy shook his head as if he could not understand. The pistol wavered, then lowered. The unreasoning fright went out of the boy's face and he dropped his head and began to cry. The woman reached out a hand toward him, then turned and threw a distraught look at Driscoll.

He knelt beside Reese. The man's shirt was open and a bandage was about the wound in his breast. The bandage was crimson with blood which trickled down to form a small pool on the floor.

"I tried," the woman said. She had the boy in her arms now, holding him tightly, while he wept with his face pressed between her breasts. "I tried all I could. But I had to keep him from coming in. I'd shoot at him behind the tank and

152

then come here and look at Noel and then back to the window to shoot again. I don't want him to die, Driscoll, not after what he did for us. Too many have died already."

Driscoll knelt there stunned, watching the faint, weary rise and fall of Reese's chest and the pale, gray look about his mouth and cheeks.

That's supposed to be me, Driscoll was thinking, me with that slug in my chest. I've squared for you, but that doesn't help any. It was my place here but I was at Half Moon making pretty talk while you were here taking the slug meant for me.

Reese stirred. The ashen lips moved a little. The eyes opened and stared directly at Driscoll and there seemed to be a plea in them, an urgent asking for something.

"It's me, Noel," Driscoll said, bending down. "It's me, Dave. Can you hear me, Noel?"

The ashen lips moved again, making no sound, not even a whisper. The eyes looked through Driscoll into something far beyond and the plea in them grew frantic.

"Noel? What are you trying to tell me, Noel?"

The lips moved again. A breath issued, like the flight of a soul. Driscoll barely heard it. For a while he thought it was the final, feeble whispering of a name, something like "Rosalie."

But afterward, he was not so sure. He was never sure . . .

The boy was quiet now and so was she. Their

tears had dried. The boy sat in a chair, still clutching the pistol and watching Driscoll with wide, wary eyes. The woman stood with her back to Reese who was covered with a blanket.

Driscoll stood at the door, watching the flies buzzing about Montana and landing on his face and on the blood on his shirt. Dusk was falling.

"You've got to go, Driscoll," the woman was saying. "You've got to run."

"You know I won't do that," he said quietly. "You know I'll never leave you and the boy until this thing is settled."

"But Longstreet will come."

"Let him."

"What if he doesn't come alone?"

He said nothing. He stood and watched the night closing in.

"I heard them talking before the fight started," the woman went on. "There was this man and he wanted Noel to throw in with him. He'd already talked Montana into it and now he was trying to convince Noel. Noel said if he ever harmed me or Billy that you'd hunt him to the ends of the earth, and the man laughed and said he'd already taken care of you. He said he'd told Longstreet he was at Bar Cross Bar when you killed Boyd and Hunter and would swear to that. So Longstreet has a warrant for you. He said there was nothing to worry about from you." She looked searchingly at Driscoll but he went on staring outside. "The way they talked, it seemed that Noel knew that man from somewhere."

"His name was Lee Fairchild," Driscoll said.

"Did you know him?"

"They were my partners, him and Noel, in that rustling I did over three years ago." Long, long ago, he was thinking, back before the world was born. "Lee never was anything but a treacherous snake but Noel was different. I liked Noel."

She was silent a moment as though out of respect for this man so recently dead. "You understand how it is, don't you, Dave? You'll go now, won't you? Before Longstreet arrests you?"

"He wants me arrested so he'll have a free hand with you. You know why, don't you?"

She nodded. "But I don't know anything. Jim never told me where he hid that money."

He stared hard at her. "Is that the truth?"

"I swear it."

He felt the pressing urgency, the need for hurry. "Then Billy knows."

He saw the sad, resigned look enter her eyes. She turned her glance away from him and stared into the long ago, living something all over again. "Yes. He knows. Jim never told me because he knew that if it ever became a question of the money or Billy's safety I'd let the money go. So he told Billy. All these years I've sort of hinted that I knew so no one would suspect him. I stayed around, pretending to be waiting for the chance to get that money. You can't imagine what it's been like for me, dreading, praying that no one would guess it's Billy who knows the secret. But I knew it couldn't last. If you've figured it out, then others will figure it out, too."

He cupped her face in a hand and made her look at him. "Do you trust me, Hazel?"

Her eyes were wide, questioning. She said nothing.

"Do you think I'm after that money? Do you think I'm trying to trick you?"

"What are you trying to say?"

"If you had that money and were away from here, then it would all be over, wouldn't it?"

A strange, taut look came over her face. She watched him without an answering word.

"Do you want that money?" he asked quietly. "Do you want it to keep and use?"

Her face clouded. There was indecision there, and pain, and bewilderment, and an old, old loss. Her fingers twined about each other.

"I can't help remembering that he did what he did for me and Billy. I can't help remembering that he died when he could have lived, even though it would have meant prison for him. He was a good and kind and gentle man. He never would have hurt anybody but he was at his wit's end and so he did what he did." Her eyes appealed to him for understanding. "He died for us, Driscoll. Don't you see? He was wrong but he died for us."

Noel died, too, for you, Driscoll thought, and I would, too, if you want that money. I'll get it for you even though I know it's wrong.

"Do you want that money?" he asked aloud.

There was horror and shame and reproach on her face but she nodded. "I do, Driscoll," she whispered.

"Then we've got to make Billy tell us."

The boy shrank back in the chair and watched Driscoll with hostility and suspicion. The woman reached down and disengaged the pistol from the boy's reluctant fingers. He looked strange and pitiful.

"Billy," Driscoll said. "I'm your friend. I was your Pa's friend, too. I only want to help you. Your Ma will tell you that."

"That's right, Billy. I trust Driscoll. You can trust him, too."

The boy's eyes held fear but they blazed defiance. "Pa told me never to trust nobody."

"I'm not like some others," Driscoll said. "I'm not trying to trick you, Billy. I want to help you and your Ma. I want to help you get that money and then I'll help you out of this range. I promise you that's what I'll do."

"He made me swear," the boy said. "My Pa made me swear. He said I was little but I was all Ma had and he made me swear to look after her. He said if he told her she would tell someone if they ever got mean with me. So Pa told me instead. He told me to wait until I was bigger, when I could look out for myself real good. He told me to wait until then before I got the money."

"Haven't I been good to you, Billy?" Driscoll asked. "Haven't I helped you and your Ma? Doesn't that mean you can trust me?"

The boy looked at him with doubt and animosity. "My Pa told me to trust nobody. He said there would be people trying to make me tell. He said some would be mean to me. He said, too, that some would be nice to me and be good to me but not to trust them, either, because they were just trying to trick me."

"Your Ma trusts me," Driscoll said, beginning to feel helpless again. "She wants you to tell me. I'm not forcing either one of you to do anything. I'm just asking you because I want to help you."

The boy shrank still more in the chair. "I won't tell."

"Please, Billy," the woman said.

"I won't tell."

"When we get to where the money is," Driscoll said, "I'll let you and your Ma take my guns. I couldn't do anything to you without my guns, could I?"

"Pa made me swear. I won't tell."

"Billy," Driscoll said, pleading now. "If you don't tell me, there will be others who will be real mean to you. Don't you understand? I just want to save you and your Ma from harm."

The boy began to weep. He beat his fists on his thighs. "I won't tell, I won't tell, I won't tell."

"Please, Driscoll," the woman said, touching him pleadingly on the arm.

"All right then," Driscoll said, knowing the galling taste of defeat again. "All right. But the two of you are going away from here. Pack a few things. Not many, just what you really need."

"Where are we going?" the woman asked.

"I don't know. I don't know just yet . . ."

They left Quarter Circle Six, taking Reese, draped and tied across his saddle, with them. Driscoll held the lead rope of the bay who followed obediently. The bay had shied when Reese had first been placed on it but the horse quickly quieted and now was quite docile.

The woman and the boy rode beside Driscoll. None of them ever looked back at the bay's grim burden. All about them was the silence of the night and of the lonely, sleeping land. The silence got its hold on them also and none of them spoke a word all the way to Half Moon.

Duchaine's dog announced their coming and Duchaine slipped out the door and stood in the shadows with a rifle in his hands. Then he saw who it was and cried out Driscoll's name.

The door opened anew and the girl came running

out. Then she glimpsed the grim cavalcade and the dead man. The girl pulled up short. Her gasp was sharp and full of horror.

Driscoll stepped down from the black. The woman and the boy stayed on their horses. In the night Driscoll could feel Duchaine's keen, querying glance. In quiet tones Driscoll told what had happened at Quarter Circle Six.

When he was through, Duchaine let out a long sigh. Driscoll watched the girl. She had glanced once at Reese, then away quickly, staring only at Driscoll from then on; and to Driscoll there came a memory, of a last, ephemeral breath, a going away into cold and darkness, a fleeing desolation and loneliness.

"Are you all right, Dave?" It was the girl's voice, low, full of tender solicitousness. He wondered that it moved him so little. "Did they hurt you?"

"I'm all right."

"Well, son?" Duchaine asked.

"I thought you might bury him," Driscoll said. "I would if I could but I don't have the time. I never knew too much about him. I heard him talk about Missouri once. But he had no real home, no kin that he ever told me about. He was a lonely man. This was as much of a home as he ever had, I guess. I think he'd like it if you buried him on Half Moon. It would make him feel as if he finally belonged somewhere."

Duchaine slapped him gently on the back. "I'll

do just that, Dave. Don't you fret none." He peered through the shadows at Driscoll. "What now, son?"

"I think we'll be riding on. Longstreet's after me with a warrant. I'll take care of Mrs. Tennant first and the boy and then see about myself."

"They're welcome here," Duchaine said. He looked at the woman. "Mrs. Tennant, I'd take it kindly if you stayed here with me and Rosalie."

"I don't think she should," Driscoll said. "You've already done more than your share. Longstreet's mad enough at you as it is. I don't want to involve you any more."

"Longstreet can't do anything to me," Duchaine growled. "I haven't done anything wrong."

"You don't have to. Longstreet's not out to preserve law and order. You know what he's out for."

There was a long silence. The horses stirred restlessly and saddle leather creaked. One of the animals pawed fretfully at the ground. The girl's eyes never left Driscoll.

"Where are you going?" Duchaine asked.

"I don't know."

Duchaine peered at him. "You can tell *me,* son."

"I haven't decided yet. I've still got to figure it out. All I know is it won't be Quarter Circle Six."

"Don't you trust me, son?"

Driscoll looked at the ground in shame and confusion. He was grateful for the darkness that concealed the emotions on his features. He had a vivid recollection of Longstreet's office and Duchaine there and knew a growing anger at his distrust of anything and everything. This doubt and suspicion had been hammered into him on the anvil of existence, out of frustration and bitterness and disenchantment, and he knew he would never change.

Duchaine sighed. "All right, son. I understand. I would do the same if I were you."

The girl said, "Dave? Could I speak with you before you go?"

He followed her over to the house and up into the thick shadows of the gallery. From here the others could not hear. She stopped and turned to face him and waited for him to come close. He could see the pale shape of her face, the winsome image it made in the shadows. The scent she used was delicate and sensuous in his nostrils.

"Dave? You think a lot of her, don't you?"

He could not on the instant find anything to say. He stood there mute and sad and remorseful.

"There isn't a thing you wouldn't do for her, is there?"

"It isn't anything like that, Rosalie. You're trying to put words in my mouth. She's alone. You saw what they tried to do to her and the boy. You saw what happened to Noel. They play rough, Rosalie, and Longstreet is the roughest and meanest of them all."

"Do you think they—the ones at Quarter Circle Six today—were in with Longstreet?"

"Montana was," Driscoll said. "Lee Fairchild could have been. You never could trust that man. You never knew which way he'd jump. Maybe he was acting for Longstreet and maybe he was acting on his own. All I know for sure is that he's framed me on a murder charge and that's all the excuse Longstreet needs to gun me down."

"Oh, Dave." She began to sob quietly.

"Please, Rosalie." He touched her gently on the arm and felt her flinch a little. Sorrow ran through him. "I can take care of myself. I've done all right so far."

"All right?" Her sobs ended abruptly. "Do you call yesterday all right?"

He winced. He'd been helpless; he probably would have been beaten to within the next to the last gasp of his life if it hadn't been for Fred Duchaine and Noel Reese. And he could not even bring himself to bare his heart to the man and his daughter. He had to heed that inner darkness, that bitter suspicion that did nothing but sour him on everything.

"I'm sorry, Rosalie."

"Today, when you kissed me, I thought maybe—" Her voice trailed off and lost itself among the shadows.

"I'm sorry," he said again. "I didn't mean for you to get me wrong. It's just that I don't aim on settling down here. When this is over and I'm still alive, I'm riding on."

"With her?"

"Rosalie, Rosalie. I don't feel that way about her at all."

"But you'd take her with you, wouldn't you?"

"I just feel sorry for her, her and the boy. And I know what they meant to Tennant. I know what he went through the last night of his life and I promised myself then that if I could ever do anything for his wife and his boy I would. That's all there's to it, Rosalie."

"You said today you'd think it over and then come to see me."

He was in the river of sorrow and reproach again. He could not understand what had led and toppled him into it. "I—I have given it some thought. You don't know what I've been, Rosalie. You don't know the men I've ridden with since I was a boy, the things they taught me, the things I've done. I've been a thief. I've been to the penitentiary because I was a thief. Now I've killed. I'm not for you, Rosalie, and you're not for me. Believe me, it's best this way."

"When you go," and her voice dripped ice, "when you ride on, will you be taking that money with you?"

He stared at her, mute. There had been cold fury in her tone.

"You *are* interested in that money, aren't you,"

she went on when he did not speak, "even though you've always pretended not to be? That's the only reason you came back here. You never cared anything at all for us here at Half Moon. It was just a place to come to when you needed help. You want that money and nothing else. That's why you want no one with you. That's why you want to ride on alone. Well, maybe you'd better then."

"Rosalie, please, let's not quarrel."

"I'm not quarreling. I'm just telling you what's on my mind."

"I'm grateful for what you and your father have done for me. I really am."

"I can see that you are."

"Rosalie, Rosalie. There will be others for you. You're a very pretty girl, Rosalie. You'll see. Someone good and fine will come along."

"No one will come along," she said bitterly. "I'll have to stay on this damn ranch all my life and grow ugly before my time. I've seen it happen to other women. What else can you expect from this damn sun and heat and wind and loneliness? That's what will come along for me. That and nothing else." She put her face in her hands and began to weep quietly.

"Rosalie." He touched her arms but she wrenched angrily away. "Rosalie. I never meant to make you cry."

"Will you come back for me then?"

"I—I don't know. I can't promise because I'm not sure but I'll think about it."

"Again?" The tears had stopped. Her voice was bitter. "Is that all you'll ever do about me, just think?"

"I've got to go, Rosalie."

"Go then."

"Goodbye, Rosalie."

She made no answer. Sadly she turned and went away. He thought she might call after him or make some sound of relenting but not so much as a whisper came out of her. He was aware of Duchaine watching him closely. Driscoll nodded curtly to the man and mounted.

He motioned the woman and the boy to start with a jerk of his head. He looked once at Reese still lying across his saddle and thought, Goodbye, Noel, for the last time goodbye. Then he touched the black with the spurs and rode after the woman and the boy.

Somewhere in the dark a night bird called, hooting and mournful, but there was no answer . . .

He hammered on the door and hammered again. Dawn was breaking and made him frantic. He could not afford to be seen, not here, not with the woman and the boy. The concealment of the night was forsaking them and the crying need right now was for secrecy. He hammered again.

Something stirred within the house, the whisper

166

of footsteps approaching the door, and he waited with his heart in his mouth, wondering now if he had made a mistake and dreading it if he had because there was no other place to fly to, not without being seen. He heard a bolt being drawn and then the door opened and Sarah Sloane was there, peering at him.

"Mrs. Sloane," he said, and saw her start when she sensed the urgency in his tone, "may we come in? All of us? I'll explain once we're inside."

She hesitated while she glanced at the woman and the boy, standing behind Driscoll. Then she stepped hurriedly back and opened the door wide.

"Of course," Sarah Sloane said. "Come right in. I have wanted so many times to ask you, Mrs. Tennant. Come in, come in."

Hazel Tennant entered with reluctance, the boy tagging along behind her. He stumbled once from weariness and the woman reached back and steadied him. He still had the pistol and the gun-belt slung over his shoulder. Driscoll followed, carrying their things, silently cursing their slowness and hesitation.

He closed the door behind him and then told Sarah Sloane what had happened. "I didn't know where else to take them," he finished. "This is the last place Longstreet would look for them. I know what's happened in the past and what this must mean to you and her and if there was any way I could take them with me I would. But I'm a hunted man now. I hope you understand, Mrs. Sloane."

While he spoke she had drawn the shades. Now she turned on him with a gentle, chiding smile. "Of course I understand, Mr. Driscoll. I would have felt very hurt had you taken them elsewhere. They will be safe here with me. No one will know they are here." She went over to the woman and embraced her and then bent down and kissed the boy. "You will always be welcome, more so than any one else, in my house."

Hazel Tennant dabbed at her eyes. The boy watched, wide-eyed with puzzlement. The need for hurry cried fiercer than ever in Driscoll.

"I've got to go," he said to Hazel Tennant, and all at once he didn't care who saw or sensed what he felt inside. He reached out and took her cold hands in his and looked deep into her eyes. "I'll take the horses with me. I can't leave them behind or someone might guess. I'd like to stay a little with you, just a little, but it's getting light outside and I've got to go before I'm seen."

He saw moisture sparkle in her eyes. "I'll never forget this, Dave. I'll remember it always. I want you to know that because this is goodbye."

"Not goodbye, Hazel. I'll still be around."

She looked at him in sudden fear. "You mean— you're not going? Dave. Where can you hide?"

"In the Sombras. They're close to Fort Britt and there are many places in them where I can hide. I will be watching this town all the time. At night

I'll come and check to make sure everything is all right. If something goes wrong and you need me, just ride toward the Sombras. I'll see you and come to you."

"Dave."

"Don't cry, Hazel." Sudden remembrance made him smile. "It seems lately that every woman I say goodbye to cries."

"I've stopped crying, Dave."

He squeezed her hands and patted the boy on the head and smiled at Sarah Sloane. Then he was out the door and once it was closed behind him his eyes began to sting. He swore at his softness, at this strange person that had taken command of him, and mounted the black and, leading the other two horses, rode westward, toward the Sombras, the mountains of shadow and sorrow . . .

CHAPTER 12

Now he knew loneliness such as he had never known before. Once his aloneness had been more of an antipathy toward his fellow men but now it was a forced isolation, an apartness against his will, a crying of yearning and a strange and sweet emotion he had never before experienced.

He found a high point on the flank of the mountains from where he could see Fort Britt, tiny and remote, in the distance. There was graze for the horses and an overhanging ledge to give him shade. He watched the land slanting and dropping below him and then rolling away into the distance.

A sense of helplessness descended on him and infuriated him. It was the idea of not knowing where to turn, of seeing evil compounded and enacted and him with his hands tied that nettled him so. Her image and that of the boy were there before him constantly. There were times when he swore softly under his breath. He checked his guns time and again just to be doing something as inaction and worry and dire speculation preyed on him.

Once he saw a dust cloud rising up from the land below and he watched with his heart picking up and banging against his ribs but the cloud was rather large and finally he made out three riders. They veered south at the foot of the mountain and were soon gone from sight.

The sun was high overhead when he saw the tiny spiraling of dust and then the lone rider racing toward the mountain. Some strange intuition told him instantly who it was and he grabbed his rifle and raced over to the black and tightened the cinches. He sent the black at a reckless run down the mountainside.

The rider was veering slightly northward, away from him, and he had to push the black hard. Caution restrained him from firing a signal shot. Caution made him ride through a grove of junipers before he sought to intercept the other. Everything in him told him it was her but he had to be sure before he revealed himself. The rider had been too distant for positive identification.

He emerged from the junipers in time to see the rider plunging up a slope above him. And he saw that it really was her and the gladness he knew was tainted with the realization that something was amiss.

"Hazel," he cried. "Hazel."

He thought she had not heard but as he was about to shout again she turned quickly in the saddle and spied him there below her. She whirled the roan she was riding so abruptly that the horse stumbled and almost fell. The roan recovered, however, and came plunging down the slope.

He saw the distress on her face, the wretchedness and fright in the wide eyes and strained mouth, and all at once pain and sorrow for her rushed at him and the great black rage that he was coming to know so well.

"Hazel," he said, dismounting and then catching her in his embrace as she slid off the roan. He held her an instant tight against him and whispered her name. "Hazel."

She pushed back from him and he could see the pallor on her face, the twitching of panic and terror in the working of her mouth.

"Billy," she whispered, seeming to look right through him into the great, terrifying distances. "Billy, Billy."

"What is it, Hazel?" he said, holding her arms, trying to get her eyes on him. "What's happened?"

"Billy, Billy."

"Hazel. What's happened to him?"

"Longstreet."

He felt the world drop out from under him. For a moment it was as though he were suspended alone in space with nothing to reach or grab or feel or stand upon. The black rage lacerated him anew.

"Longstreet?" he echoed. "He found you at Sarah Sloane's?"

The woman nodded.

"But how? I'm sure no one saw us. I'm very sure of that. I'm sure, too, Longstreet never could have guessed. Not so quick, anyway. How come he found you so fast?"

"I don't know," she moaned. "He's got Billy, Dave, Longstreet's got Billy."

"What happened?"

"It was horrible, Dave." She dropped her head and began to weep brokenly. "It was horrible."

"You've got to tell me," Driscoll said, shaking her. "You've got to tell me so I'll know what to do."

"He made Billy tell."

"How? He wouldn't tell me, not even when you begged him to." He felt the rage and the hate grow blacker and deeper and more virulent. "Did he hurt the boy? Is that how the old sidewinder made Billy talk?"

"He never touched him," she said. "It was me. Billy wouldn't let him hit me any more."

He looked at her. In the haste, the worry, the anxiety he had not noticed the bruise on her cheek and another high on her forehead. Malevolence spawned in Driscoll. Brutality snarled in him.

"All right," he said, surprised at how quietly he spoke when he was so aflame inside. "Longstreet's gone after the money then?"

She nodded jerkily. "He took Billy with him because he said if I told anyone, if anyone went after him, I would never see Billy again." Her frantic eyes beseeched him. "Did I do wrong coming to you, Dave? Did I do wrong?"

He put a hand gently on her cheek. "No, Hazel. Have you told any one else?"

She shook her head.

"Does Sarah Sloane know?"

She nodded. "She tried to stop Longstreet but he hit her, too. He was like a crazy man, Dave. When he wouldn't stop hitting me, when he said he'd hit me until I was dead, Billy broke down and told."

Driscoll had a searing recollection of the chain shrieking and the blows raining and felt the blackness darken in him still more.

"Do you know where Longstreet went?"

She nodded again. "It was a map that Jim had made. I didn't see it but Longstreet in his excitement said a name."

"Where was the map?"

"You know that pistol Billy was always playing with? He would never part with it but I thought it was because his father had given it to him, the last present he ever made to Billy."

"The map was in the pistol?"

"No. In the gunbelt. Jim made the map, took the slugs and powder out of some of the shells, tore the map up in small pieces and put a piece in each shell, then put the slugs back."

The dark animal moved in Driscoll. "What was that name Longstreet said?"

"Ladron." Her eyes searched his face anxiously. "Does it mean anything to you?"

174

He smiled slightly, without mirth, only in bitter memory. "Ladron Canyon."

"It's here in the Sombras," she said. "Do you know where?"

He nooded grimly. "I know the Sombras well. It was my business once to know them very well. I know all the canyons and hidden places there are to know. Ladron Canyon isn't a stranger to me."

She clutched his arm, fingers digging urgently. "You'll be careful? He said he'd hurt Billy if anyone went after him. You'll be careful for Billy?"

"I'll be careful."

"Could—could I come with you?"

He smiled gently and stroked her cheek. He shook his head. "It's best I go alone."

"Where will I wait for you?"

He had to think a moment and hastily consider all that was involved and would become involved. "Better make it Quarter Circle Six. I'll come there first of all."

"Goodbye, Dave."

"Don't worry too much, Hazel."

He kissed her softly, tenderly, on the edge of her mouth and found her lips come seeking his. He broke the embrace quickly and mounted the black and rode away. He did not trust himself to look back . . .

The vultures wheeled and banked against the sky with the endless, foul patience of their kind. Death is a long wait and they knew and so they sailed on rigid wings while on the earth below things died and became carrion.

When Driscoll spied them, he felt his heart squeeze within the clasp of a hand of ice. Billy, he thought, then put the dread thing out of his mind. It could be a dead cow or wild animal attracting the vultures and the fact that they still soared indicated that whatever lay on the earth beneath was still alive.

He sent the weary black on cautiously. The walls of the ravine he was following reared sharp and tall on either side. Water had once washed the floor of the ravine and still did when occasional cloudbursts came. Now the floor was dry and barren, however, the dust of waste and time covering it.

The first thing that warned him was the sudden rising of the vulture from its perch on the limb of a dead tree. It flew off with a great, foul flapping of black wings and then Driscoll saw the horse and after that the man.

The horse stood alone with empty saddle. It whinnied when the black appeared and the black answered. The horse tried to move toward them but it kept stepping on the trailing lines and that stopped it. It tossed its head and snorted nervously.

The man lay on his side with one arm extended out in front of him as though pointing a way up the ravine. A breeze stirred the thinning, sandy hair and ruffled his shirt about the shoulders. Driscoll thought the man to be dead until he saw a leg flex slightly, then still again.

Duchaine, Driscoll thought, and felt pain and sadness lance through him.

The man's weapons were gone. His holster was empty and when Driscoll glanced at Duchaine's dun he saw the saddle scabbard was empty, too. Blood formed a carmine pool beneath Duchaine.

He rolled Duchaine gently on his back. Crimson ran from the wound in Duchaine's breast. Death was weaving its gray mask over the man's features. He sighed, deep and weary, and the breath clogged once in his throat with a rattle. Then it cleared and the man's eyes opened and looked up at Driscoll.

The eyes focused slowly and a frown appeared on Duchaine's brow as though what he saw puzzled him. Then recognition came. "Ah, Driscoll," he whispered.

The dark animal in Driscoll crouched on its haunches. "Longstreet?" he growled.

Duchaine nodded once, weakly.

"What were you doing here?" Driscoll asked.

"We followed you," Duchaine whispered.

Driscoll frowned. "Followed me? When? Where?"

Duchaine's mouth worked soundlessly twice. He sucked in a breath and that seemed to restore his voice. "Fort Britt. We followed you there. Oh, we were very careful. We read your sign. I was a tracker once, a scout, in my Army days. I remember once—" He broke off and with an effort brought himself back to the present, painful things. "We kept out of sight. You never once suspected. We tracked you, all the way to Sarah Sloane's house."

"We?" Driscoll said, puzzled. "You and Longstreet?"

"Not Longstreet. Rosalie."

It seemed as though mention of her name revitalized Duchaine. He came up on an elbow, reaching out with his other hand, pawing, grabbing at the air. "Rosalie?" It was a great, sharp shout, torn achingly out of him. "Rosalie!"

Driscoll put an arm about Duchaine's shoulder. "Easy, Duchaine," he said. "Everything will be all right. I'll look out for Rosalie. If Longstreet's harmed her—"

"Harmed her?" Duchaine choked and spat blood on a vicious laugh. "I'd been better off if I'd never fathered anything." He clawed at Driscoll with a hand. "I would have tracked you. I would have reasoned with you. If nothing else had worked, only then would I have got tough with you. I would have waited but she was tired of waiting. She left me and went to Longstreet."

Driscoll listened, stunned, sick, filled with disenchantment. He had always been right about the world after all. There was no goodness, no compassion, no charity or mercy. There was nothing but duplicity and treachery and conniving and deceit.

"Everything I've ever done was for her," Duchaine went on, gasping and struggling over the words. "There wasn't a thing I wouldn't have done for her. She was always dreaming of being a great lady. She had big dreams and so I promised I'd help them come true. Maybe because she was all I had when my wife died. All I had—and now I find that I'm the father of a monster."

He coughed and a bloody froth bubbled on his lips. He wiped it away with the back of a hand. "Because I had promised to help her, I played up to you. I pretended to be your friend. I offered you a job, my home. She did her part, too. Don't look so bitter, son. You're young and if you live you'll be hurt again, but once if you're lucky, many times if you're not.

"We figured you knew where that money was or if you didn't that you'd get the secret out of Mrs. Tennant. So we watched you, Driscoll. We watched you well. But I wouldn't have used violence on you unless there was no other choice. I'd have been patient. But she was in a hurry so she threw in with Longstreet. Damn her and her memory. May she die with him and go all the way to hell with him."

"Duchaine," Driscoll said, able to speak again. He could feel the sour running of the bitterness in him and the disillusionment. But there was another thing worrying his mind, a greater, stronger, fiercer thing. "The boy. How is the boy?"

A blankness was coming into Duchaine's eyes. His anger had sapped his strength. He sagged heavily in Driscoll's arms and his voice was a whisper again.

"What boy?"

"Billy Tennant." Panic brushed Driscoll. "Doesn't Longstreet have him with him any more?"

"I never saw the boy. I never saw anyone. Longstreet bushwhacked me."

"Didn't you see anything at all?"

"No. The bullet hit me and everything went black. I came out of it laying on the ground and hearing his spurs coming at me. You never forget Longstreet's spurs. I couldn't move. I had to lay there, not even breathing. I could feel him looking at me and wondering if he should put another slug in me to make sure. Then he bent down and all he did was take my pistol. Then I heard him walking away. There was no boy. But I know she was with him. I never heard her and never saw her. But I could feel her somewhere there, watching and not caring, even though I was her father. May she burn in hell. May she burn in the hottest part of it."

"Forget her," Driscoll said gently. "Think of yourself, Duchaine. Make peace for yourself."

Duchaine's fading eyes searched Driscoll's face. A faint smile touched the dying man's mouth. "There's not much time, is there, Driscoll?"

Driscoll shook his head.

"You're honest with me. I like that, Driscoll. But I'd have known anyhow. I can feel it in me. I'm sorry for anything I might have done to you. I wish— Would you give me your hand, Driscoll?"

Driscoll caught the errant, groping fingers and squeezed them. Duchaine smiled the last smile.

"Thank you, Driscoll," he whispered, and died . . .

He found the tracks of three horses heading deep into the Sombras. On the moment he knew elation, and then the blackness came over him. Three horses. One for Longstreet. One for Rosalie Duchaine. One for the boy?

He searched the sky ahead fearfully but there was nothing, just the immense blue, no wisp of cloud, no birds of carrion floating with their ominous patience. He looked back once and searched that part of the sky and that was empty, too. Sorrow came to Driscoll, and remorse.

I'm sorry, Duchaine, he thought, but I had no time to bury you. If I live, on my way back. But I've got to get to the boy. You understand, don't you?

He emerged from the ravine and followed the tracks across a tiny bowl secluded here in the mountains. The peaks seemed to rear ever higher, more forbidding. The air held an abysmal chill as though it had come all the way from the far, frigid corners of space. He kept the black at a steady lope.

The sound came from the left of him, from behind some thickets. The black heard it, too, in the same instant and shied, snorting in fright and nervousness. Driscoll whipped out his pistol and held it thrust out in front of him, and, just as he was about to quit the saddle to flatten himself on the earth it came to him that the sound was that of weeping.

Dread moved darkly in Driscoll. He sent the black ahead. Driscoll's every sense was alert. His hand grasped the pistol tightly. He felt his lips draw back from his teeth in a silent snarl. The weeping stopped abruptly and he heard a small, sharp cry of alarm and then he was through the thickets and could see.

She had been sitting on a rock and was just starting to rise when Driscoll came in view. The moment he appeared she stood upright quickly and gave a small shriek of relief and gladness. Her hands reached out beseechingly toward him and the tears began to pour anew down her face.

She was wearing a buckskin divided riding skirt and a bright red shirt and a plaid jacket. He imagined that she must have looked very pretty in the outfit before the skirt got soiled and the jacket got torn in two places. Her face was red and her eyes were swollen from crying. There were dust smears on her cheeks where she had sought to brush away the tears with her fingers.

"Dave, Dave," she wept. "You don't know how I prayed it would be you. Dear, sweet Dave."

He had reined in the black and she came up to him and folded both arms around his leg and pressed her face against his thigh. Her shoulders shook from the violence of her weeping.

Nothing moved in Driscoll. He sat in the saddle, staring down at her without pity, without reproach, without any feeling.

She sensed this indifference and her face lifted swiftly, staring wide-eyed up at him. The tears had stopped again though their wetness glistened on her lashes and on her cheeks.

"Dave?" she said, voice small and quavering. "Dave? You haven't said a word. What is it, Dave?"

He holstered the pistol now. She still clung to his leg as she stared up at him. There was a touch of the frantic in her grip.

"I found your father," he told her quietly. "He's dead."

She made a hoarse moan. Her face worked. "Oh, it was horrible, Dave. You can't imagine how horrible it was. Longstreet shot him without a warning. He shot him and left him and made me go with him until he got tired of me and left me here. I prayed that you'd come. God heard and answered me."

"You'd better pray for yourself. You need it."

"Dave?" Her face appeared to pale under a dawning realization. Her voice became a horrified whisper. "What are you saying to me, Dave?"

Now he began to experience a bit of anger, of loathing. It made his voice a trifle sharp. "Your father wasn't dead when I found him. He died in my arms. He died cursing you."

She released her hold on him as though he were something repugnant and foul. She stepped back and put both her hands over her face, holding herself there tightly. The blue eyes grew very wide with panic and horror. Finally she took her hands away. Her fingers left white marks on the redness of her face.

"Dave," she said, her voice pleading. "Dear, sweet Dave. Please try to believe me. There was nothing I could do. There's nothing anyone can do with Longstreet. He's insane. If I'd said one word against him he'd have killed me. Don't you see? He left me here to die."

"How come you were with him in the first place? You didn't go unwillingly with him then."

"He made me go. Didn't I tell you once how he tried courting me? He used me and then cast me aside. I swear it, Dave."

"You went to him to begin with. You told him about the Tennants being at Sarah Sloane's."

"No," she cried. "That's a lie, Dave."

"I have your father's dying word on that, Rosalie."

Her hands clenched, then opened. She looked about her, at the barren, jagged peaks, the lonely desolation, the sense of distance and lostness. A wildness entered her eyes and she began to weep anew.

"Dave, Dave. I was jealous. I was crazy with jealousy. When you rode away with her, when you preferred her to me, I went out of my mind." She shook her head frenziedly. "I never meant to. I didn't know what I was doing. I love you so much I can't stand the thought of losing you. I wanted to hurt you. So I went to Longstreet and told him. That's the only reason."

She stood staring up at him, waiting for his answer, but he did not speak.

"Once I'd told him," she went on, "I was sorry. But it was too late then. So I went with him. Because he had the boy. I wanted to make up in some way for what I'd done so I went with him to look after Billy. Don't you believe me?"

"How is Billy?"

"He's all right. He's very frightened but he's all right. Longstreet hasn't hurt him yet."

Yet, Driscoll thought and felt the frantic urgency sweep at him. He started to turn the black away. As he did so, the girl ran in and seized the black's bridle, stopping the horse.

"Dave?" she cried, voice hoarse with horror. "Aren't you taking me with you, Dave?"

He looked down at her coldly. He could feel

the pounding of a pulse in his temple. "There's no room for you. I've got to think about Longstreet and the boy. I can't burden myself with anything else."

"I wouldn't get in the way. I love you, Dave. Please take me."

"Even if I could I wouldn't."

It was as though he had lashed her across the face. She jerked back, paling, but she still clung to the bridle.

"Dave," she said, whispering her fright and terror. "How am I going to get out of the Sombras? He took my horse. I've got nothing. No horse, no food, no water. What will I do?"

"You'll have to walk."

"But I can't, Dave. Dear, sweet Dave. It's too far."

"I turned your father's horse loose. I took off the saddle and bridle and put them beside your father. You can walk that far. You might be able to track and catch your father's dun. If you can't then you'll have to walk all the way."

"Won't you be coming back this way? You can't cross the Sombras from here. You'll have to come back this way."

He felt a gloom come over him, a premonition of the grave, darkening his spirits a moment, filling him with an instant's futility.

"I don't know if I'll come back. I don't know where my trail will end. Let the bridle go, Rosalie."

"No." She grabbed it with both hands, pulling the black's head down. "No. I'll never let go. You've got to help me."

Wrath surged in him, making him shout. "Let go, Rosalie."

"No. I love you, Dave, love you, love you."

"For the last time, Rosalie."

"No."

He struck the black hard with the spurs, harder and crueler than he had ever struck the animal, and his heart ached when the black squealed in pain. But the horse lunged ahead, despite the dragging weight on the bridle. Driscoll struck again and the black squealed once more and lunged again, violently, and the girl's grip broke.

She shrieked as she fell and the black broke into a run. She shrieked as she scrambled to her feet and started running after the racing horse. She shrieked anew as she stumbled and went sprawling in the dust.

Then she knew that she was lost. And she began to scream curses after him . . .

He kept the black at a hard run until he was sure he could no longer hear her shrieks and curses. He slowed the black to a lope then and his eyes were wet as he bent down and patted the black's sweating neck.

"Forgive me, boy," he whispered. "Forgive me."

The black gave a small, soft whinny. It trotted

on, the dust cloud not so big behind it now. The noise of its hoofs was the only sound in the vast, solemn stillness of the Sombras . . .

Ladron Canyon.

He smiled once, briefly, more with bitterness than with mirth, when he thought of the name. Ladron. A Spanish word meaning "thief, robber." It was a most appropriate name, he told himself.

He had been here once, back when the world was young and he had only fancied that he'd experienced disillusionment and sorrow; now the world was old and he was old and bitter with it. He had been here with Noel Reese and Lee Fairchild—they seemed long dead and very distant in his mind all at once—to scout the canyon as a hiding-place for the cattle they had planned on rustling. But the canyon had been too barren. There was no graze, no water, only crags and ledges and crevices and old, old caves. They had explored one of the caves and found a skull and pottery and a piece of rusting armor. Nothing else. So they had abandoned the canyon in their plans.

He had the tracks to guide him, the tracks of three horses. Billy, Billy, he thought time and again. If he's harmed you I'll make him wish he'd never been born. I'll think up tortures that even an Apache couldn't dream of if he's harmed you.

He rode cautiously now, scanning the bleak,

forbidding walls, the crags and ledges, the clusters of boulders. He rode with every sense keen and alert, with his heart beating a steady, hard rhythm, with the dark animal poised ready to spring in the darkness within him. He watched the black's ears, every twitch of them; he could feel the thump-thump of the horse's heart against his legs.

There was a curve in the canyon wall here, veering sharply to the right so that he could not see around it. The wall rose steeply. A ledge was tacked to it and from here it was possible to ride up a sharp slant to the ledge. He remembered that beneath the lip of the ledge there were several caves carved in the rock by the elements and the ages.

He saw the black's ears perk up. He reached down swiftly, clamping a hand over the black's nostrils before it could whinny. A wind was blowing down the canyon, carrying some scent to the black and carrying their own away.

All at once Driscoll had a feeling, a certainty, something that told him it had to be thus and no other way. He did not know exactly what had to be thus. It was just a sensing, like knowing suddenly that it's your turn to die. A cold breath touched him briefly. A breath of the tomb?

He sent the black up the incline to the top of the ledge. The black's hoofs dislodged a couple of stones and they went rattling down. Driscoll held his breath and strained to hear something, anything that the wind might tell him lay ahead. But he could not translate its urgent whispers. He had to proceed alone, on his own.

The black rounded the bend. Here the ledge was very narrow, just enough room to pass, and for several awful moments he was outlined starkly against the sky, a tempting target for anyone below. Then the black moved on and here the ledge widened considerably so that it was possible to conceal himself from below by riding close to the canyon wall.

The black seemed to sense Driscoll's tenseness, the need for quiet, and it was putting its hoofs down gingerly and quietly. Driscoll saw its ears twitch sharply and he reached down again to cut off a nicker. He could feel the horse straining beneath him, the quick, strong thumping of its heart, its striving to go ahead toward the edge of the ledge though he held it back.

The ledge was not high here and the caves were below. Was this the place then? His heart began to run swiftly as he pulled his pistol and then inched the black ahead with his knees. He was bent forward in the saddle, toes hard against the stirrups, straining everything to see or hear, and then, just as he had vision of the ground below, a horse called from there.

He saw Longstreet and the boy in the same instant. The boy walked close beside Longstreet who was carrying a pair of soil-stained saddle-bags. Their backs were to the ledge and Driscoll and they were walking toward the three horses standing with trailing lines not far away, but the instant one of the animals whinnied Longstreet spun, hand streaking for his pistol.

"Run, Billy, run," Driscoll shouted, and then fired.

For the boy's safety he had to aim for Longstreet's side, away from the boy. Driscoll's aim was quick and bad. He missed the ribs but the slug smashed into Longstreet's right forearm as he was raising his sixshooter. The gun fell from Longstreet's nerveless fingers but before Driscoll could aim and fire again, Longstreet dropped the saddle-bags he'd been carrying in his left hand and reached for the boy.

The boy had come around and was standing there, transfixed with surprise and fright. His bulging eyes looked up at Driscoll. The boy's mouth gaped. His face was pale and racked with terror.

In a flash Longstreet was down behind the boy and sweeping him tight against him with his left hand. With those fingers he clutched the boy about the throat and began to squeeze.

"Who do you want, Driscoll?" Longstreet shouted up at the ledge where Driscoll sat on the black, all helpless now. "Me or the boy?"

Defeat cried in Driscoll. He could no longer

shoot, not with the boy held so close and Longstreet crouched down on his knees behind Billy, peering up at Driscoll with a fierce, maniacal look on his long, cadaverous face. Longstreet's hand squeezed tighter about the boy's throat. Billy gasped and his eyes bulged and he began to claw at Longstreet's fingers but could not dislodge them.

"Me or the boy, Driscoll?" Longstreet cried, all caught up in madness and greed and insensate fury. "I'll choke him. I'll strangle him to death if you don't throw down your guns."

Driscoll could have wept. Lost, lost, a voice wailed in him, all is lost. He watched with pain and horror as Longstreet's fingers closed tighter.

"First your pistol, Driscoll," Longstreet shouted. "Off the ledge and here in front of me."

"Give the boy a breath, Longstreet."

"The pistol first."

The sun flashed off blued gun metal as the pistol dropped. Something went out of Driscoll then, something that he was sure could never come back.

"Let the boy breathe, you sidewinder."

"All right. One breath." The fingers loosened and the boy took one great, gasping breath. Then the fingers tightened anew, cruelly, inexorably. "Now your saddle gun. Right here alongside your pistol. Hurry it up, Driscoll."

The rifle made a soft, rasping sound as Driscoll

drew it out of its saddle scabbard. Hazel, Hazel, he thought achingly, I've let you down, Hazel. I only hope he keeps his word and doesn't harm Billy. But I know what Longstreet's word is good for. The rifle turned end over end as it fell and then landed with a soft plop beside the pistol.

Longstreet laughed, a sound of triumph and evil joy. "Hah. Not a bad trade, hey, Driscoll? The boy for all this money?"

"Damn you," Driscoll cried, raging. "Let him breathe."

Longstreet gave that laugh again. His Stetson had fallen from his head and dangled down his back from the chin thongs and his tawny hair looked like the glistening hide of a panther in the light of the sun. His face threw a mocking jeer up at Driscoll and then Longstreet laughed once more.

"All right, Driscoll," he said, and loosed his fingers. The boy began to take great, gulping breaths. The sound of his gasping reached up to the ledge. "You stay right there, Driscoll. Don't you move a finger."

Longstreet's right forearm and hand were dripping blood but he released the boy with his left and then swiftly clutched him in a tight embrace with his right. A spasm crossed Longstreet's face but he hung on tightly to the boy. With his left hand Longstreet picked up his own pistol and Driscoll's and shoved them into his waistband.

He grabbed the rifle and tossed it awkwardly over by the horses. Then he picked up the saddle-bags in his left hand.

"If I so much as hear your horse move, Driscoll," Longstreet said, his face all savageness now, "the boy gets it. I'll bash his head against a rock. You hear me, Driscoll?"

"When you gonna let him go?"

"When I'm good and ready. I need him a little while yet."

"You dirty low-down snake."

Longstreet grinned, the puma grin. "You call me one more name, Driscoll, and the boy gets it. Understand?"

Longstreet rose slowly to his feet, carrying the boy in the crook of his right arm and the saddle-bags in his left hand. He began to back toward the horses.

Driscoll's heart was banging like a drum. Urgency cried loudly in him. How? How? he frantically asked himself, and all but wept when he heard no answer. He bent forward in the saddle to watch better, with anguish, with despair, and it was then that his fingers touched the lariat hanging from his saddle horn and in that instant the idea and the plan was born.

Longstreet tossed the saddle-bags across his roan. Then he transferred the boy to his left arm to boost him up on the horse. He was not going to let the boy ride his own mount. For a moment

Longstreet's back was turned and in that instant Driscoll snaked the rope out and down.

The loop was small. Longstreet sensed it coming but before he could whirl the noose was already dropping over his head. He let the boy fall. Billy cried out in pain and fright. The roan shied up against the other horses and they wheeled and snorted in startlement and confusion. Driscoll gave a yank to the rope just as Longstreet was reaching for the noose.

With two good hands he might have succeeded. As it was the fingers of his left hand just barely touched the noose and then it had closed tight about his neck. Driscoll ran a dally around the saddle horn and jabbed spurs in the black, wheeling him away from the lip of the ledge.

He saw the rope go taut and stay taut. The cinches squealed and the saddle strained as the black backed. From below came the sound of a gasping, a rattling, and he knew that by now Longstreet's feet must be off the ground. The black had reached the canyon wall and could back no more.

Then metal began to sound, the ring of Longstreet's spurs. He was not suspended above the mouth of a cave but against solid rock, and he strove desperately to find some purchase against the rock. He sought to drive his heels into some tiny depression or catch hold of some small nob but his long-shanked spurs foiled him. He could not use his hands for his back was to the rock and he could not turn. The fingers of his left hand rose and clawed at the rope biting into his neck. The nails dug crimson trenches in the flesh of his throat. Twice he raked himself and then the hand fell. The spurs grew silent. The mouth gaped in the soundless, everlasting cry of death . . .

He sighted the buildings of Quarter Circle Six in the dim, gray light of dawn. The boy had been all worn out from grief and fright and exhaustion and had not been able to sit in his saddle. So Driscoll had taken him on the black with him and the boy slept now in his arms.

The wind blew cold off the flanks of the Sombras and Driscoll hunched his shoulders to better protect the boy from its chill gusts. A strange wonder and enchantment filled Driscoll as he looked down at the sleeping boy. It was a sensation Driscoll had never experienced and it left him with a sweet, cloying ache in his throat.

She had not slept at all that night and had been outside since the first pale streaking of the dawn, straining her eyes toward the Sombras. Now she made them out, the one rider with something in his arms, and the second horse trailing behind with empty saddle.

She gave a scream and went running toward them. She stumbled once and fell and for a moment was out of sight among the tall grama.

Then she was up again, running toward them, laughing and crying all mixed together.

"Billy," Driscoll said gently. "Wake up. You're home."

The boy roused, blinking his eyes and looking about drowsily. Then he heard his mother's voice, crying his name over and over, and the last mists of sleep fled from him and he struggled out of Driscoll's arms and slid to the ground and went running toward the woman.

She swept him up in her arms with a glad and anguished cry. She hugged him to her and wept and he wept with her. Driscoll walked the horses in and sat, staring down at them, all at once unmoved by what he saw. A breath of the old darkness passed over him and he knew sadly that not all had been settled.

She let the boy down now and looked up at Driscoll. "Thank you, Dave," she whispered. "Oh, thank you."

He knew his face was grim. He took the saddle-bags and dropped them at her feet. She looked at the saddle-bags and then at him, eyes wide with puzzlement.

"There's the money," he said quietly. "I told you if I could I'd get it for you. I'll even help you leave this range with it if you want me to. It's not what I think is right but I'll do it anyway."

She was watching him with a strange look on her face. He drew a breath and went on. "I can't

197

forget that your husband died for it. I won't ever forget what he went through just so you and the boy could have it. I'm not saying he was right but it's what he gave his life for and so I've brought it to you. But other people died because of it and it makes me wonder."

Fresh tears glistened in her eyes. Her lips moved but no sounds emerged. So he went on.

"I don't have anything at all but I'm willing to work hard for you and the boy. I won't ever steal or kill for you. That is a part of me that is dead now and will never come alive. But I'll be good to you and him, as good as I know how. But I won't rob or kill." He drew another breath and it made a small sound like a cry. "If you want to keep the money, it's yours, but I want no part of it. I'll help you again if you need me and want me to but I won't ever share in that money."

She picked up the saddle-bags and held them up to him. Her eyes were shining. "Here, Dave. Take the money. Do with it as you wish. Take it to Sarah Sloane. It's really hers. Take it to her and then come back. Come back to Billy—and me. . . ."

Center Point Large Print
600 Brooks Road / PO Box 1
Thorndike ME 04986-0001 USA

(207) 568-3717

US & Canada:
1 800 929-9108
www.centerpointlargeprint.com